Reign of Terror

Buffalo hunter Woodrow Clayton experiences the full horror of the Comanche terror at the Battle of Adobe Walls, and then again in the bloody aftermath that spreads along the frontier. He vows to help the US Army put an end to it, once and for all.

Homesteader Jared Tucker sees his wife and son slaughtered, and daughter, Lucy, carried off by Comanche raiders. From then on he is solely obsessed with rescuing her.

Together, the two men travel to Fort Concho and persuade Colonel Mackenzie of the Fourth Cavalry to let them accompany his expedition against the infamous Comanche half-breed war chief, Quanah Parker. Unfortunately for them, Mackenzie has far greater priorities than the recovery of one thirteen-year-old girl. So it is left to Clayton, Tucker and a bloodthirsty Tonkawa Scout to take their private war on to the 'Staked Plains' of West Texas in search of the wretched captive.

Reign of Terror

Paul Bedford

A Black Horse Western

ROBERT HALE

© Paul Bedford 2019
First published in Great Britain 2019

ISBN 978-0-7198-2995-6

The Crowood Press
The Stable Block
Crowood Lane
Ramsbury
Marlborough
Wiltshire SN8 2HR

www.bhwesterns.com

Robert Hale is an imprint
of The Crowood Press

The right of Paul Bedford to be identified as
author of this work has been asserted by him
in accordance with the Copyright, Designs and
Patents Act 1988

Typeset by
Derek Doyle & Associates, Shaw Heath
Printed and bound in Great Britain by
4Bind Ltd, Stevenage, SG1 2XT

AUTHOR'S NOTE

Setting aside the tricky ethics involved in the American Indian Wars of the nineteenth century, there can be no denying that the warfare waged by the Comanches against pretty much all comers was certainly the longest, and possibly the hardest fought, in North American history. It is also a fact that the man credited with finally ending the ghastly catalogue of death and misery was Ranald Slidell Mackenzie. Anybody curious about this extraordinary soldier would do well to investigate his career, because a mostly fictional novel like this can hardly hope to do it justice.

CHAPTER ONE

The screaming apparitions had apparently come out of nowhere, but every single buffalo hunter and merchant in the trading post of Adobe Walls had immediately recognized them for what they were. That first attack at dawn came close to overwhelming the twenty-eight desperate defenders, who had been forced to fight at close range with revolvers and repeating rifles. They would have fought quite literally with tooth and nail if necessary, because all realized the sheer horror that defeat would bring. And so, somehow, they had survived, with only three fatalities endured . . . so far.

The various buildings that made up the isolated commercial venture just north of the Canadian river, in the Texas panhandle, were not actually constructed of adobe. That was because the original settlement that had given the place its name was now nothing more than ruins. Most of the present structures were made from prairie sod, which was a very good thing, since such material was all but impervious to fire.

Now, on the third day after the initial assault, the siege continued its bloody course, which in itself was quite amazing. Hitherto, no Comanche war party had been known to besiege a fortified enemy. Yet everything about this ferocious engagement had been different. The number of warriors involved, for a start. Including Kiowas and Southern Cheyenne, there were many hundreds painted for war, which was greater than at any time since the 1840s . . . and they seemed prepared to accept casualties. Not even the wounding of the pre-eminent war chief, Quanah Parker, had brought it to an end.

But Woodrow Clayton had a fair idea why so many Indians were trying to kill him. He and his avaricious compadres were only the latest and worst of a long line of threats to confront the plains tribes. Cruel and combative by nature, the proud horse warriors were being brought to their knees by a combination of, to them, mysterious diseases, and the white man's relentless slaughter of their food source, the buffalo. And so, after a period of fragile peace, the Comanches and their allies had responded in the only way they knew. They were out for blood, and more particularly scalps, prisoners and horses.

'They're on the move again!' bellowed a young fellow going by the improbable name of Bat Masterson.

And they were, too. An awful lot of them. Nearly naked except for assorted breechclouts, their bronzed bodies daubed with ochre and vermilion, they swept in with terrifying speed. Nearly every one of them carried a heavy buffalo hide shield, though mercifully such things were no defence against a well-aimed Sharps rifle with virtually unlimited ammunition.

Clayton and a young shaver called William Olds were hunkered down together on the roof of Rath and Wright's store, their powerful long guns cocked and ready.

Olds spat a black stream of tobacco juice over the edge prior to remarking, 'You'd think those God-damned savages would've given up on this foolishness by now, wouldn't you?'

Any reply was lost in the crash of gunfire, as both men fired almost simultaneously. Even as other shots rang out from nearby buildings, Olds let out a whoop of delight. One of their assailants had toppled from his pony just in front of their elevated position, blood pumping from a mortal wound. The Indian lay in the dust, helplessly twitching in his death throes.

As the familiar whiff of sulphur reached his nostrils, Clayton swiftly worked the under-lever of his weapon and slid another long, expensive cartridge into the breech. Although most people's money would have been on him, he couldn't have said for definite whose bullet had done the killing, and he didn't really care. On that first desperate day, his hands had trembled with fear, but no such reaction occurred now. He and the others had come to realize that so long as they remained behind cover and kept up a hot fire, they would likely survive. And thankfully, the very nature of their employment meant that they had brought thousands of cartridges with them. If anyone was going to run out of ammunition, it sure as hell wouldn't be any of the hide hunters!

The Comanches weaved between the low buildings at great speed, both controlling their ponies and shooting a mixture of firearms with breathtaking skill. It was not for nothing that they were considered by some to be the finest light cavalry in the world. But as was usually the case, they failed to utilize their far greater numbers and press home the attack.

'Pile it into them,' someone yelled from the roof of the nearby makeshift saloon.

'I'll do de telling,' bellowed out the Irish proprietor, James Hanrahan, from the room below.

Many of the defenders at ground level were now using revolvers to maintain a high rate of fire, which resulted in clouds of powder smoke hanging in the still, dry air. Rapid shooting at fast-moving targets meant that no more attackers were brought down, but the sustained defence soon had the warriors high-tailing it back to the elevated ground in the north-east. The white men then returned to their 'buffalo guns' to encourage the withdrawal. It was then that Olds abruptly jumped up and headed for the wooden ladder leading down from the roof.

'Where the hell are you going?' Clayton queried.

'It was my bullet felled that bastard, and I aim to get me his scalp!' the eager young man retorted.

'Don't be a fool. They might not be finished,' Clayton protested, but his cautious claim was ignored.

With one hand still clutching the cocked rifle by its forestock, Olds swivelled sideways, so as to get a foothold on the ladder. Cursing at such recklessness, his companion anxiously searched for any sign of a renewed attack. What happened next would have taken anyone by surprise.

Acutely nervous despite his apparent bravado, the youngster had only descended two rungs when the Sharps' trigger snagged on the outer edge of the ladder's rail top. With the muzzle barely inches from his skull, the powerful gun discharged with a terrible crash and burst it like a melon. As blood and brain tissue sprayed over the horrified Clayton, Olds lifeless body fell backwards on to the sun-baked ground like a rag doll.

Startled defenders in the adjacent saloon saw the corpse slam to earth in front on them. 'Sweet Bejesus, who was dat?' Hanrahan demanded twitchily. He genuinely thought that the Indians had fled out of range, but you never could tell with those devils.

Clayton sighed despondently. For Olds to have survived the siege, only to die by his own hand was just too cruel. 'Kilt by his own gun,' he yelled over. 'Got careless, I guess.'

The saloonkeeper grunted something unintelligible, before adding, 'An' are dem Comanche gone, or what?'

Clayton, having mopped some of the gore from his face, took a good long look before answering. 'They is an' they ain't. There's a bunch of them sitting their ponies on that bluff off to the north-east. I reckon it must be close on a mile from here.'

Following that news, the beleaguered occupants of

11

Adobe Walls cautiously came out into the open. It was as Clayton had said. There was no immediate threat, just a continued brooding presence.

'Well, dat just tears it,' Hanrahan exclaimed. As a businessman, he had more pressing matters on his mind than just fighting pesky Indians. 'Dere's been more than enough hunting and drinking days lost. It's high time dem sons of bitches left for good, and dere might could be a way to encourage dem!'

'What you thinking on, Jimmy?' a certain Billy Dixon enquired. Like a lot of the hunters, he was young and cocky, with scant respect for his elders.

The other man scowled. 'I'm after thinking on how you should be calling me Mister Hanrahan,' he replied sharply. Then his manner softened slightly. 'You reckon you could maybe knock one of dem heathens over from here? Show dem that they really should be moving on.'

Even as some of the others guffawed at such a ridiculous notion, a smile slowly spread across Dixon's unshaven features. After all, killing critters at long range was his business.

'That's one heck of a tough shot,' he cheerfully acknowledged. 'But it sure would be something, wouldn't it?' So saying, he raised the ladder sight on his Sharps and began to contemplate the vast distance involved. As was always the case when adjusting it, he had to take into account windage and elevation. Scooping up some dust, he let it fall and observed how little it was affected by the elements. Thankfully, the sun would be behind him, and therefore highlighting his prospective victim. Glancing around, he spotted the remnants of an adobe wall that would provide support at the right height. Moving over to it, he selected a cartridge from the bandolier around his chest.

'How many grains you using, Billy?' queried one of his companions with professional interest.

'One hundred and ten,' the other responded. 'That much powder would put a big shaggy down . . . even at such range.'

'If you could hit it,' another commented. 'Aim for one of their ponies, why don't you? That way you'd at least bring something down.'

As he carefully took up his position on the wall, Dixon favoured him with a wry smile. 'I ain't no horse killer, Sam.' With that, he tucked the rifle butt into his shoulder and retracted the hammer. Peering intently down the barrel at the distant figures, he chose one who was directly facing the settlement, with the full width of his torso to aim at. It occurred to him that he'd taken on one hell of a task. The unsuspecting savages were mere flyspecks. Then again, his rifle was known as 'the gun that shoots today and hits tomorrow'.

Such was the concentration involved that all emotion drained from his face. Even his breathing had to be strictly controlled. With so vast an expanse to cover, the slightest error as the heavy lead bullet left the barrel would result in a hopeless failure. Near misses counted for nothing on the unforgiving frontier.

Squeezing on the first of the double set triggers meant that the second required only the slightest touch, and as he suddenly held his breath, that was exactly what it got. The Sharps was a weapon of outstanding precision, and as it discharged with a tremendous roar, Billy Dixon instinctively knew that he'd done good. And yet, as he stared intently at the tiny figures, there was no movement of any kind. Then one of the warriors jerked, as though hit by a mallet, before sliding off his pony and lying still. His painted companions milled around in obvious confusion, unable to comprehend what had just happened.

A great hurrah went up amongst the assembled hide hunters. Experienced marksmen, they all knew exceptional shooting when they saw it, and so every single one of them recognized that they had just witnessed something truly remarkable.

Even the habitually cynical Hanrahan was impressed. Thoughtfully scratching his bristly chin, he offered his opinion 'Dat was mighty well done, me fine boyo. I'll be after giving you a drink on de house, an' no mistake. Dere can't be no one ever took a shot de like of dat before.'

High praise indeed, but the marksman was having none of it. 'Thank you kindly, Mister Hanrahan. But I'd have to call it a scratch shot, 'cause I don't think there's any way I could ever repeat it if I lived to be a hundred!'

Nonetheless, his audience's noisy jubilation was only compounded when the remaining Indians turned away and hurriedly rode out of sight. That was all the confirmation they needed that the bloody siege, which in time would come to be known as the Second Battle of Adobe Walls, was finally over!

'We've given them hard knocks here,' Woodrow Clayton asserted. 'It's set them back, an' they're gonna be mad as hell.'

'So?' Hanrahan demanded impatiently, glancing around at his other clientèle. Most of them were enthusiastically celebrating their miraculous survival . . . and that suited him just fine.

With the Comanches and their allies apparently gone for good, it was high time they all started earning some money. After all, wasn't that why they had travelled all the way from Dodge City in the first place? Their avowed intention was to kill and skin as many buffalo as possible, and then haul the hides back to the railhead there.

'So, they'll look for easier targets,' Clayton persisted grimly. 'Settlers with families an' such, to butcher and torture. We've got to spread the word along the frontier. Warn the army.'

'To hell with dem bluecoats,' the other man scoffed. 'An' to hell with settlers too, I reckon. Anybody coming into this Godforsaken country needs to be able to look out for demselves, like we done. Besides, we got buffalo to kill, an' cash money to make.'

Clayton regarded him askance. He knew full well that the Irishman never got his own hands dirty. He just offered up his watered-down 'rot gut', and lived off the labours of others. And yet it wasn't that that bothered him.

'You just don't get it, do you? We only stood those scalp-lifters off because we were all together, behind walls. If we split up and get to hide hunting again, they'll pick us off in ones and twos, out in the open. None of us will ever see Kansas again ... and you won't make a penny piece, 'cause you won't have any customers left. We need protection out here, just like everyone else. Which is why we need the army.'

The grasping saloonkeeper still wasn't convinced. Conspiratorially lowering his voice, he gestured towards his sorry-looking premises and stated, 'Everything I own in the world is in dis building. And with dat bit of magic from young Billy, dem bastards won't be coming back here. It's my chance to score.'

Sadly, Clayton finally accepted that he was just wasting his time. The Irishman, motivated solely by avarice, was simply blind to the reality of the situation. And so, without uttering another word, he turned and walked away.

'Sure, an' you're a fine man, Clayton,' Hanrahan called after him. 'Just be careful it's not your own bones dat end up bleaching in the sun!'

At first light the following morning Woodrow Clayton mounted up and headed south. On hearing of his self-imposed mission, several men had wished him well, but nobody was there to wave him off. Not quite believing that the Comanche horde had actually gone, those hunters still sober had passed a fitful night, so that most of them were now trying to get a few hours shuteye.

His intention was to reach Fort Concho, warning any white folks that he should encounter on the way. He had been told that thankfully there was an experienced commander on the frontier, who possessed the ability to tackle these murderous savages. Well, he would believe that when he saw it. Because for decades, due to the lack of political will and funding, the army had been forced to fight with one arm tied behind its back, allowing the Comanches and Kiowas to subject Texas to an unmitigated reign of terror. Just how bad it would get this time was anybody's guess!

CHAPTER TWO

Jared Tucker never felt entirely easy about being absent from the family cabin, but there were occasions when he just couldn't avoid it. He had cattle to tend to and water sources to check on. And it was also an undeniable fact that he enjoyed his occasional lonely sojourns far out beyond the tenuous settlement line, even when there was no real need for them. As a salve to his conscience, he told himself that there hadn't been any news reaching them of Indian trouble during all their time living next to the Brazos river. And yet, always in the back of his mind, there was that little niggle eating away at him. What if?

Folks back east had chided him for taking his family out on to the Texas frontier, but he had felt a great yearning for the wide open spaces to be found beyond the confines of so-called civilization. He had had a bellyful of what civilized people were capable of. It was also a fact that once the twenty-eighth state had finally been subdued, great opportunities would open up for those already there. And again, as he kept reminding himself, the four of them had been in residence for over a year, and he hadn't yet clapped eyes on a single dreaded Comanche. Perhaps, as was so often the case in life, their reputation for savagery had been overblown to frighten errant children.

Reining in his horse, the lone settler stared around him at the seemingly limitless terrain. There was a raw beauty to it that never failed to captivate him. He knew that some men would find the vast emptiness daunting, whereas for Tucker the solitude acted as a balm to his troubled soul. The awful horrors that he had witnessed during the War of Secession had remained with him, and would doubtless do so until the end of his days.

The former reluctant conscript was a tall, raw-boned man of thirty-six. He carried with him a self-contained air that some people found off-putting, but was just a product of his unusually constrained eastern upbringing. None of this affected the profound love for his wife and children that he frequently demonstrated and that stayed with him on his forays.

He blinked rapidly, as though coming out of a trance, and for a moment felt only confusion. The animal beneath him was pawing the ground restlessly, and he really had no idea just how long he'd been sitting there lost in thought. The sun had certainly moved on, and he realized with a start that he needed to be making his way home . . . immediately. One rule he always stuck to was to return before dark. Wheeling the suddenly eager horse around to face east, Jared Tucker urged it into a trot. The thought that his wife,

Grace, and two children, Samuel and Lucy, would undoubtedly start to worry about him created pangs of guilt that were not entirely unfamiliar.

'God damn it all to hell!' he uttered aloud, and repeatedly dug his heels into the horse's sides.

The dying sun was beginning to slip below the horizon by the time the lone horseman approached the final rise before the Tucker homestead became visible. A smile of anticipation spread across his good-looking features. Even just a single day's absence was enough to bring a tightness to his chest at the thought of seeing his family again. Glancing up from beneath his wide-brimmed plains hat, he spotted the lone pine that acted as a beacon. Then his eyes narrowed, as anxiety replaced eager expectation. The pall of smoke rising behind the tree was far more than any cooking stove might produce.

A single shot crashed out, which Tucker instantly recognized as belonging to the old Spencer that he had given to Samuel. The two things together could only mean one thing . . . serious trouble.

'Dear God!' he exclaimed, dragging the 'Yellow Boy' Winchester from its scabbard. Frantically beating his startled mount with the barrel of it, they raced to the crest of the rise. As the cabin and its outbuildings came into view, Jared Tucker's worst nightmare suddenly became a reality.

There was too much to absorb in total, and so he seemed to focus on individual snippets of horror that would never leave him. Young Samuel frantically trying to work the Spencer's lever action, as some painted savage fired an arrow into his belly. Lovely Grace, spread-eagled on the ground, and straddled by the lustful assailant cutting her dress away. Delightful Lucy, so full of life and fun, standing before the smoking cabin, screaming her lungs out in terror.

There were maybe a score or more Indians in the raiding party, but Tucker never hesitated. Howling with rage, he levered up a cartridge and urged his tired horse down the slope. Charging headlong towards the cabin, he saw Grace's attacker rip the final remnants of clothing from her. She offered no resistance, as though having already been beaten senseless. The warrior's intention was obvious, and it was simply too much for Tucker to contemplate. Swiftly pointing his Winchester with one hand, he snapped off a shot. Having deliberately aimed high to avoid Grace, there was no real hope of actually hitting her attacker. He just wanted to claim the bastard's attention.

The bullet kicked up dirt a few yards away from his wife, causing her would-be rapist to glance up from his pleasurable task. That individual obviously decided that he was under deadly threat, because to Tucker's absolute horror he abruptly drew his blade sharply across her throat. As Grace's lifeblood spurted into the air, her husband thought that he must be going mad. Oblivious to his own safety, he continued his rapid approach, and levered up another cartridge. This time, he precariously relinquished his hold on the reins and aimed directly at her murderer. With the distance closing all the time, Tucker fired.

The bullet slammed into a bare chest, tearing through bone and tissue. With blood gushing from the fatal wound, Grace's killer uttered a great moan and collapsed on top of her unresisting body. A collective howl of anger rose up from his companions, as they all turned to face the fast approaching rider. One thing was for sure: Jared Tucker had now most definitely attracted their attention!

With the boy screaming in agony and the girl screaming with fright, their father had no intention of reining in. He was in the grip of an uncontrollable bloodlust that took no account of personal danger. Yet it was also true that the Comanches had no intention of letting him get any closer. At least half a dozen firearms crashed out, and his horse went down as though it had been pole-axed.

Without any warning, Tucker found himself flying through the air, but the sensation was only fleeting. He struck the hard ground with a bone-jarring thump that entirely knocked the wind from his body. If the Indians had rushed him then, he would have been finished, but thinking him already dead they turned their attention to his children.

Samuel was hysterically tugging at the arrow excruciatingly wedged in his belly. Blood coated the whole of his store-bought checked shirt. Fourteen years old, he was on the verge of manhood, but still able to cry like a baby. A number of the warriors dismounted, and advancing on him in a semi-circle, began enthusiastically to taunt his pathetic efforts. Behind him, the cabin was still smoking, but had resisted the

Comanches' attempts to burn it down, because although framed with wood, it was mostly constructed of prairie sod.

Desperately sucking air into parched lungs, Tucker groggily rolled over and struggled to his feet. Every part of his body felt as though an anvil had hit it, but amazingly, he didn't seem to have any broken bones. And if nothing else, the fall had knocked some sense into him. He recognized that charging wildly at so many opponents would achieve nothing. Glancing around, he saw his bloodied horse lying unmoving on the ground. Instinctively he staggered over to the large cadaver and dropped down behind its protective bulk.

One of Samuel's gloating tormentors had just seized hold of the arrow's feathers when an unexpected shot rang out. The bullet struck him between the shoulder blades, pitching him forwards on to his young victim. With mixed howls of anger and dismay, all the Comanches returned their attention to the solitary white man, barely visible behind his flesh and blood rampart. One of the Indians who had remained mounted was quite obviously their leader. He wore a thoroughly grim headdress, consisting of the scalp and thrusting horns of a bull buffalo, which endowed him with an unforgettably menacing demeanour. Gesturing angrily at those others of his warriors who were still mounted, he barked out a guttural command. Reacting immediately, they launched themselves towards their deadly foe.

With both his children in plain sight, Tucker was

suffering the torments of the damned. His every instinct told him to rush to their aid. Yet he knew that the only chance of survival for any of them was for him to fight off the raiding party. As though emphasizing his dilemma, there was a meaty thunk as another bullet struck the carcase of his horse. As the shrieking Comanches closed in, he suddenly recalled what a Union sergeant had once said to him in the late war:

'Don't ever scare, Tucker. ' 'Cause if'n you do, you're dead for sure!'

Drawing a fine bead on the nearest marauder, he squeezed off a shot. As the lead tore into bronzed flesh, he then shifted his aim and smoothly worked the under-lever. Under normal circumstances it made sense to move position after firing, but on this occasion he simply had nowhere else to go. Even as his bloodied victim toppled to the ground, Tucker fired again with similar results. Although he, too, was under fire, the bullets struck his barricade harmlessly.

Seeing two of their comrades struck down so rapidly was too much for the remaining warriors. They habitually didn't like taking casualties, because by their reckoning that made warfare painfully unproductive. Far better to strike hard and fast, and then move on with any plunder that they had managed to seize. With consummate skill, the mounted warriors split into two groups and veered off to either side, desperate to get clear of the lethal sharpshooter. Their leader shouted out another command to those still afoot. It was time to leave. No longer able to torture the wounded boy at leisure, the disappointed savages abruptly shifted their attention to the terrified girl.

Unable to drag her eyes from the bloody mess that had been her mother, Lucy had so far been rooted to the spot. Yet with the shocked realization that she was now their sole prey, the pretty thirteen-year-old frantically raced for the illusory safety of the smoking cabin. She barely made it to the threshold before claw-like fingers roughly seized her hair and dragged her off her feet. This time, Lucy's pitiful cries were pain induced, and they easily carried over to where her father lay hidden.

The heart-rending sounds cut through him like a knife, and he ached to rush to her aid. Yet logic told him that no good would come of it. He was still vastly outnumbered and on foot. As he had recognized earlier, her only chance was for him to stay alive. He couldn't even fire at his daughter's captors, for fear of hitting her. All Jared Tucker could do was watch as the jubilant warrior, surrounded by his cronies, dragged her to a pony. Unceremoniously tossing the wailing girl on to it, the Indian then leapt aboard behind her and urged the animal up to speed. The horrified parent did the only thing that was left to him.

'Stay alive, Lucy,' he bellowed out. 'I'll come for you. Just stay alive!'

At that moment, the war chief suddenly reined in and stared intently at him for a few seconds. Then he raised the lance in his right hand and pointed it directly at the white man. As a sardonic smile appeared on his harsh features, the Comanche shook his head emphatically before turning away. Digging

25

his heels in, he moved off at speed, herding the riderless ponies ahead of him, thereby ensuring that the impotent Texan had no immediate chance of following them.

Tucker momentarily contemplated 'popping a cap' on him, but then the sight of his supine son banished such pointless thoughts from his mind. Long gun at the ready, he cautiously got to his feet. It was very apparent that the men he had shot were dead, and so he hurried over to Samuel. Reaching him, he dragged the warrior's corpse away from the boy, and then shuddered at what he saw. His beloved son was quite obviously beyond any help. The arrow was still wedged in his belly, and his pants were literally drenched in blood. Samuel's eyelids flickered slightly, and suddenly he stared up at his pa with feverish intensity.

'Oh Christ,' was all Tucker could manage. Taking a knee, he tenderly clutched the boy's hand.

Samuel drew in a few short, sharp breaths and then was abruptly and irrevocably still. It was as quick and final as that.

Oblivious to his own bruised and aching body, Tucker was engulfed by an uncontrollable rage that caused him to roar after the departed war party. 'I'll slaughter every one of you sons of bitches for this. Just see if I don't!' With that he slumped forwards, so that his tear-streaked face touched that of his dead son.

How long he remained like that he would never recall, but then with a start it came to him that Samuel was not the only dead member of his family. Guiltily, he drifted over to Grace's naked body in an almost trance-like state. Had the Comanches returned at that moment he would have been easy meat.

Dropping painfully to his knees at her side, he dreamily stared at the once beautiful woman for long moments, before gently closing her eyelids with his fingers. Overwhelmed with cumulative grief, he didn't even register the arrival of darkness. With the horrors that lay about him, it was as though his very soul had descended into such a state. Whatever the new day held for him, Jared Tucker would greet it as a much-changed man!

In the same amount of time that it might have taken to eat a hearty meal with her parents, Lucy's whole world had been turned upside down . . . quite literally. Although in shock from seeing her mother savagely murdered, the whole thing seemed like a nightmare that she wasn't being given the chance to wake up from. A short distance from the cabin, her foul-smelling captor had come to an abrupt halt. She had then been dragged from his pony and flung face down over one of the spare animals. Crying out in protest, the girl was quirted savagely across the back and but-tocks, and then her hands and legs were roughly secured under the pony's belly with strips of rawhide. The bonds were so tight that every subsequent move by the creature seemed to be stretching her arms in their sockets.

Now, as every passing moment took her further away from her pa, uncomprehending despair swept over the thirteen-year-old. Unable to see, and barely able to breathe with her face pressed against the animal's flesh, she had only her hearing. But brief snatches of incomprehensible conversation gave no clue as to what was to happen to her. With her flesh still stinging from the whipping, she surrendered to floods of tears, but strangely they didn't last long. With no one to offer soothing words, or even show the slightest interest, there seemed little point in continuing with them.

The young girl had no idea where the Indians were taking her, or what they would do with her when they got there . . . which was perhaps just as well. And so, all Lucy was left with were those few words of hope: 'I'll come for you. Just stay alive!' Since she knew that her pa never lied to her, this meant that once he had obtained a new horse he would surely be following on. All she had to do was be there when he arrived. So with a child's logic, sweet Lucy decided to make friends with the strange men who had taken her. But it would only take until the end of their journey for her to discover the total futility of such a plan!

CHAPTER THREE

As he had dreaded, Woodrow Clayton's journey had already proved his theory about the likely aftermath of the fight at Adobe Walls. Resolutely heading south, without encountering a single living soul, he had just forded the Red River when he came upon the first butchered corpse. It had once been a man, but by then was just a piece of bloodied meat, fit only for the inevitable scavengers. With everything of value removed, the remains gave no clue as to the reason behind its doomed presence on the southern plains. Clayton didn't even dismount. Instead, he allowed his nervous animal its head, and they left the gruesome scene at speed.

His next encounter occurred close to the Pease river, and in its way was even more shocking. Here he came across an empty, burnt-out wagon along with three mutilated cadavers. From the number of livid puncture marks in the flesh of two of their number, they must have resembled pincushions until their thrifty assailants had extracted the arrows for future use. What particularly distinguished this from his previous discovery was that one of the poor unfortunates had obviously been captured alive, and then horribly tortured over a lengthy period of time. Tied to a wagon wheel, the prisoner had been suspended over an open fire until his head had become hideously charred and distorted. He must have been a long time dying, and despite Clayton's lack of religious beliefs he found himself making the sign of the cross over the ruined corpse, but only after he had vomited the contents of his stomach into the long grass. It occurred to him that such ferocious warfare allowed no latitude for give and take, and that if ever there was a strong chance of his being captured, it would be far better to end his own life with any weapon he might have to hand.

Although their animals and belongings had been taken, Clayton had discovered a couple of spent Sharps cartridges. From these, he surmised that the men had most likely been hide hunters, which also possibly explained the horrendous torment that had been meted out. He well knew that not all of them had congregated at Adobe Walls. Some men just naturally preferred to keep clear of larger, more regimented groups. From the lack of other bloodstains in the immediate vicinity, it appeared that they had been caught completely by surprise. He didn't even bother searching for the distant corpses of any buffalo. Those creatures' tongues were undeniably delicious, but he had temporarily lost his appetite, and in any case the Indians had probably already butchered anything found out there.

Again, the lone horseman opted to move steadily on, his Sharps canted across the saddle horn ready for instant use. Twice more that day he spotted distant plumes of smoke, but there was no accompanying gunfire, and Clayton had no desire to go looking. His stated intention was to warn those still living, rather than waste valuable time and effort burying the dead. It was also a fact that the longer he remained in one place, the more vulnerable he became, and his gruesome discoveries had badly shaken him.

The only time he actually stopped again in daylight was at the Pease river crossing, where he drank his fill and replenished his canteens. He would perhaps have been interested to know that he was within spitting distance of a battle of some fourteen years earlier between Comanches and Texas Rangers that had resulted in the rescue of Cynthia Ann Parker, one of the first white children to be abducted on the Texas frontier. Eventually marrying one of her captors, she became the mother of war chief Quanah Parker, recently injured at Adobe Walls. Having lived with the Indians for twenty-eight years, her enforced return to her natural family had ended in a predictably sad outcome.

Moving on refreshed, Clayton got well south of the river before stopping for the night. Necessarily passing the hours of darkness in the long grass, he kept a cold camp, feeding on biscuit and pemmican, before sleeping fitfully with his horse's reins tied to the saddle horn next to his head. The following day would find him approaching the Brazos river, and he felt genuine trepidation at what he might find on that leg of the journey. Had he possessed second sight, Clayton might well have turned east and headed for Fort Sill instead!

As was their custom following a murder raid, the war party had ridden hard and fast through the night. And always they travelled west, initially close to the Brazos, and then next to the North Fork, sometimes referred to as the Salt Fork, of that same river. Only when their leader finally felt that they were secure from any pursuit, however unlikely that might be, did he signal for them to rein in. By this time Lucy was barely conscious. So much so that she wasn't even aware that they had stopped, until the rawhide bindings were cut and she was dumped on to the hard ground. She lay there insensible, until someone laughingly kicked her in the ribs. Perversely, it was then that she became aware of the awful pain in her extremities, as the circulation began to return. Whimpering miserably, the terrified girl slowly opened her eyes. The first rays of light were appearing in the eastern sky, just sufficient for her to take a look at her captors. Nothing that she saw gave her any comfort.

Under Lucy's immature scrutiny, the fearsome warriors appeared to possess no redeeming features. Every one of them was almost naked, and coated in animal grease. Their bursts of speech, uttered around mouthfuls of cold food, were completely unintelligible to her. Then she got her first good look at the war chief. Gazing in stupefied horror at the buffalo scalp and horns, she was unaware that her jawed had quite literally dropped. Only when it was too late did she realize that he had seen her staring at him. His seemingly cruel lips twisted in a mirthless smile and then he leapt to his feet. As he advanced on her with a strangely rolling gait, Lucy frantically tried to stand up. In truth, he and his ilk looked far less impressive when dismounted, but such considerations meant nothing to her. As her numbed legs gave way, sheer terror overwhelmed her. How could anyone appear so fierce?

The Comanche peered down at the pitiful child, but felt absolutely no pity whatsoever. Without warning, he suddenly lashed out with his right foot, catching her squarely in the face. Every man present could hear the sound of bone breaking in her nose.

As her head seemed to explode in agony, Lucy again collapsed to the ground. High-pitched wailing filled the air, until she began to gag on her own blood. Quickly tiring of the entertainment, the chief barked out a guttural command. Her captor loudly guffawed his appreciation, then seized her by an ankle and dragged his pathetic victim back to the waiting pony. With blood pouring from her now deformed nose, she was barely even aware of being flung aboard and having more rawhide tied to already painfully sore wrists and ankles.

Sadly, it would have been of no solace at all to know that thus far she had actually got off very lightly, compared to most freshly apprehended female prisoners of these justly feared southern plains Indians!

Wisps of smoke on the horizon first alerted Clayton to some kind of human presence ... and the untold danger that could represent. Although he was definitely not looking for trouble, it was also the case that this latest discovery was directly in his path, and he was feeling decidedly shame-faced at having ignored two fires the previous day. Consequently, he approached the Tucker homestead with both caution and determination. On drawing closer, Clayton realized that the smoke wasn't coming from a chimney, but rather the cabin itself. The timber frame had pretty much gone, but the intense heat from it meant that the sod walls had continued to smoulder. His throat was abruptly parched, as he realized that this could only mean further Indian activity.

Then he saw bronzed bodies lying in the open, and suddenly, from around the side of the building, a tall figure appeared. The man was white, and carried a long gun in one hand and a spade in the other. Immediately everything became terribly clear.

'Hello by the cabin,' Clayton croakily hollered. 'I'm white same as you, an' no threat.'

Taken by surprise, Tucker dropped the spade and swung the Winchester up to cover the unknown rider, retracting the hammer as he did so. He remained silent, and there was an intensity to his gaze that was mighty unsettling.

'Sure would be a shame to kill the only other living white man in these parts,' Clayton remarked evenly, somehow managing to sound a whole lot calmer than he felt.

Tucker cocked his head slightly to one side, as though puzzled by such a claim. 'How could you possibly know that?' he abruptly demanded.

The other man drew in a deep breath. 'Because riding down from just north of the Canadian, all I've found so far is dead bodies. Got no reason to think it'll be any different elsewhere.'

Tucker's eyes widened slightly, and slowly he lowered his weapon. Then, gesturing back to two freshly dug graves, he replied, 'It isn't!'

'Kin?' Clayton asked warily, as he eased out of the saddle.

The settler blinked rapidly, as though waking from a dream. 'Some,' he allowed with wretched sadness. 'But not all I possess.' His rifle was suddenly aimed directly at the newcomer. 'Which is why I need your horse!'

It was Clayton's turn to blink. Now standing next to his animal, he held the Sharps loosely in his right hand ... which wasn't really a whole lot of good. Nevertheless, he decided to play a hunch.

'Seems like something mighty bad's occurred here, but there's no call to make it worse, mister.'

Tucker's forefinger noticeably tightened on the trigger. There was madness still raging within his skull that made him very dangerous indeed. 'Drop that cannon and step aside, or I will surely kill you,' he snarled.

The hide hunter swallowed hard. There were beads

of sweat on his forehead that bore no relation to the heat. He was scared, just like he had been when the Comanches first attacked. And yet there was something else as well. Stubbornness. No stranger was just going to ride off on his horse, leaving him afoot in what was now indisputably hostile Indian country. So instead of complying, he stood his ground and took a huge gamble.

'What's her name? The one they took.'

Tucker blinked with surprise at the entirely unexpected question. He had anticipated fear or hostility, not conversation. 'Lucy. Her name was – is – Lucy. She's only thirteen years old, and I'm all she's got left.'

Clayton nodded. 'Well, I've just come from a big fight with a great horde of Comanches at a place called Adobe Walls. We managed to give them a bloody nose and stand them off, but others might not be so lucky. I agreed with myself that I'd warn the army at Fort Concho, and that's what I aim to do. Unless, of course, you kill me. But then a lot of innocent folks might die on account of that. Is that really what you want?'

For the first time, hesitation appeared on Tucker's anguished features, and the rifle muzzle wavered slightly. 'But I have to get her back somehow,' he blurted out.

Clayton sighed. 'Yeah, you do,' he agreed. 'But you can't do it all on your lonesome. You don't even know what tribe they are, or where they're headed. Double up with me and come to the fort. If we can persuade the cavalry to go after Lucy, I promise I'll go with you.'

That was one hell of a commitment, and he knew it. But there was something about this whole desperately sad situation that had touched his soul.

Tucker's shoulders sagged slightly as he finally lowered the gun. 'You'd do that for me, after all this?'

The other man favoured him with a genuine smile that had nothing to do with his continued survival. 'Yeah . . . yeah I would. For the same reason that I'm making this journey, which ain't just about being a good citizen. If people like me are ever gonna make a chunk of money out of this land, it needs to be made safe.' He glanced sadly at the two fresh graves. 'And men like you should be able to raise their families in peace as well.'

Tucker's tired face finally registered the makings of a smile. There could be no denying the sincerity of what he'd just heard. 'What's your name, mister?'

'Woodrow Clayton. My friends call me Woody.'

Something else had just occurred to the homesteader. 'How did you know it was my daughter that had been taken?'

The hide hunter shrugged. 'A hunch. From what I've heard, Comanches have a fondness for carrying off females. Even if they don't keep them for their own uses, white girls can fetch plenty in trade down in Mexico. Which is why she'll still be alive. If you keep that in mind, it might help you some.'

Tucker stared at him contemplatively for a few seconds, before nodding. 'Well then, Woody. Looks like you and me's headed for Fort Concho!'

*

Their progress had been necessarily much slower than Clayton had been used to on his solitary journey south, because in reality two big men couldn't ride one horse for any distance without killing it. Consequently, it took the whole of that day to reach the Clear Fork of the Brazos. And when they did, it occurred to him that it was a powerful shame that they couldn't somehow avoid all of the many rivers in Texas, because every time he approached one he encountered a bloody mess.

There was one big difference with this latest confrontation, in that it was still taking place! The harsh sun had changed into a great red ball as it descended on the horizon, and its beauty seemed an incongruous backdrop to the rattle of gunfire. As the two men drew nearer, they could also hear the pounding of hooves and a great deal of incomprehensible shouting. The fight was taking place where the terrain gently fell away towards the river, so that the combatants were still out of sight.

It had been Clayton's turn to ride. Slipping out of the saddle, he remarked to his companion in a somewhat unnecessary whisper. 'I guess we'd better take a look-see. You might get a chance to kill some more Comanches.'

The mild attempt at humour was completely lost on Jared Tucker. His features were drawn and intense at the prospect. 'I didn't come to Texas to kill folks. There was enough of that back east. All I want is my Lucy back.'

Clayton sighed. It occurred to him that there were

times when he just didn't know when to keep his trap shut! Ground tethering his animal with a picket pin, he muttered, 'Don't pay me no mind, Jared. Sometimes I've just got rocks for brains, is all.'

Together, but apart, they edged forward to the crest of the slope. An extraordinary sight greeted their eyes. Seven massive box wagons, with mule teams attached, had ground to an enforced halt directly before them on the northern bank of the watercourse. Several freighters were on the ground next to the vehicles in varying states of bloody distress, although from their activity none of them seemed likely to die. One man had an arrow in his thigh, but was bawling at his companions to get moving.

'If you stay here, you're all dead, you lazy bastards!'

Sadly, lack of effort had little to do with it. The ubiquitous Comanches had timed their attack to perfection. Killing the two lead mules of the team just as they were about to enter the water had stopped the front runner in its tracks. The others could have attempted to cross elsewhere, but by then the freighters were all fighting for their lives. The safest refuge was under the wagon beds, which was from where some of the survivors were mounting a desperate defence.

Whilst a number of the horse Indians pressed the attack with gun and bow, others were weaving around the stalled wagons with amazing agility, hacking at the traces to free the mules. Such was their speed that not one of them had even been injured by the return fire.

'So what do you reckon?' Tucker asked, as the two

men lay prone in the grass. There was a glint to his eye that suggested he'd already made his decision. Although the absence of the chief with the conspicuous buffalo headdress meant that this had to be another band of hostiles, he now possessed an implacable hatred of all and any Indians, which was a sadly all too familiar emotion for most frontier folk brutalized by violence.

Clayton had also weighed up the situation. 'I reckon that if those bastards run the mules off, there'll be little chance of getting the wounded to safety.' He paused for a moment, before offering his suggestion. Patting his Sharps, he stated, 'I've got the perfect gun to whittle them down a bit, but if they turn on me it'll take that repeater of yourn to hold them off. Are you up for it?'

Tucker didn't even have to consider it. 'Damn right I am!'

The two men crawled away from each other on all fours, until a good few yards separated them. Then the buffalo hunter peered down the barrel over open sights and drew a bead on the nearest fast-moving pony. Although most of the large creatures he normally shot at were stationary, they were also at vastly greater distances, so the trade-off pretty much guaranteed his success. And sure enough, as the rifle crashed out, the pony's front legs buckled, throwing its rider clear over its head.

Before the startled Comanches could react, Clayton had replaced the spent cartridge and was already lining up another victim. Again his 'big fifty' belched forth death, and again a bronzed rider was thrown at the hard ground with stunning force. It was only then that both the Indians and the freighters realized that another party had entered the fight.

No attempt at concealment could hide the telltale powder smoke. Consequently, a number of warriors wheeled their ponies about and raced directly towards Clayton's position. Only then did Tucker open up with his 'Yellow Boy', so nicknamed because of the bronze/brass alloy used in its construction. Working the lever action like a berserker, he sent a stream of lead towards the fast approaching Comanches. Such was his speed that only one of them was hit, but the rapid fire proved too much for the disconcerted Indians. Caught by surprise and dismayed by the abrupt change of fortune, the whole war party simply turned and fled. It did not escape Tucker's notice that they galloped off in a north-westerly direction . . . just as had those that attacked his homestead.

Cautiously getting to their feet, the two men waved at the relieved freighters, receiving a resounding 'huzzah' in response. As Clayton went back to retrieve his horse, Tucker reloaded his Winchester, collected the spent cartridge cases and then warily moved towards the wagons. He well knew that his companion's bullets had struck horseflesh rather than humans.

Sure enough, close to the stricken ponies, he spotted two half-naked figures in the grass. One had obviously sustained a broken neck, and was quite dead. The other lay helpless, uttering some kind of

41

mournful chant, as he favoured a painfully broken leg. Ignoring the approaching freighters, Tucker gazed at the Comanche with vengeful loathing. Up to only a couple of days earlier he hadn't encountered even one of them before, yet now he hated the entire race. And so he resorted to something that he would never have considered possible. Cold-blooded murder. Staring into a pair of defiant, obsidian eyes, he abruptly levelled his Winchester and fired. The bullet struck the injured man just above his top lip, killing him instantly in a welter of blood and gore.

The first freighter to reach him, a big fellow with smallpox scars, grinned broadly. 'You fixing on taking his scalp, mister?'

Tucker stared at him in surprise. Even now, such a thing would never have occurred to him. 'I don't want anything they have, except my daughter back.'

The other man registered good-natured bemusement. 'Suit yourself.' So saying, he drew his knife, knelt down and began to saw away at the Comanche's scalp. He was obviously new to such work, because it took some time before the bloody trophy came away in his hand. 'I ain't never had me one of these afore,' he proudly announced.

As Clayton appeared on horseback, one of the other freighters waved him over to the wagons. 'We're mighty glad you fellas showed up when you did,' he hollered, his relief plain to see.' And once they were close enough to clasp hands, he added, 'Name's Giddings. Josiah Giddings. I'm in charge of this outfit.'

After responding with his own name, Clayton

glanced down the line of heavily loaded wagons. 'Where you fellas headed with all this?'

'That there's corn, amongst other things,' Giddings readily responded. 'We're on our way to resupply the Fourth Cavalry at Fort Concho.'

Clayton's eyebrows rose in surprise. 'Hot dang! That's where we're going; only with one mount between us it was taking a mite longer than it should. Mind if we tag along?'

The other man nodded eagerly, but any chance of further conversation was swiftly curtailed by a deal of wailing from the unfortunate with an arrow in his thigh. His companions abruptly lost all interest in dead Indians and gathered around. They soon determined that the head would require cutting out . . . but not just yet.

'After it's out, the wound's gonna need cauterizing,' Giddings opined dubiously, as he hunkered down next to the suffering man. 'Problem is, for that we'd need a fire and time, which we ain't got. Those varmints might still be out there, an' we need to get the wagons rolling. So it'll have to wait until we reach the post surgeon at the fort. I'm right sorry about this, Lester,' he added apologetically.

Now falling under the influence of a copious amount of whiskey, that man shrugged fatalistically. 'Yeah, yeah. Well at least plug the damn bleeding, you lily-livered sons of bitches!'

And so they did. They also snapped off most of the shaft, which brought forth such a scream that not a man present didn't shudder and wish that he, too, could likewise get drunk.

CHAPTER FOUR

'Don't take this the wrong way, 'cause we're all mighty obliged to the both of you, but we'd kind of admire to know what brung you fellas on to this trail,' Giddings remarked, as they all sat on the grass within the circled wagons. 'Only there ain't much of anything on offer in these parts.'

Having crossed the Clear Fork of the Brazos, they had continued travelling until well past nightfall. Even then, having put many miles between them and the ambush site and desperate for some hot coffee, they all agreed that a cold camp was for the best.

As though temporarily relieving themselves of a burden, the two men graphically related their stories. Tucker's in particular elicited commiserations but no surprise, from men well used to the trials and tribulations of the Texas frontier. Although choking with emotion, he finished his tale with the firm avowal, 'So once Woody has told what he's seen, I'll be demanding help from the commanding officer to find Lucy!'

Even in the gloom, Giddings' change of expression

44

was evident. 'A word to the wise, mister. Nobody demands anything from Colonel Mackenzie. He's one hell of an Indian fighter, but he's also the coldest son-of-a-bitch you'll ever meet. Look crossways at him, an' he'll throw you in the guardhouse an' swallow the key.'

'Well, after what I've seen since leaving Adobe Walls, he's gonna have to at least listen to us,' Clayton retorted. 'Because there's a reign of terror on this frontier, an' that's no error.'

Despite his pre-occupation, Tucker's eyes widened in surprise at the somewhat flowery language. 'Where'd you learn such fancy American, Woody?'

That man shrugged. 'I ain't always been a hide hunter. My ma and pa made sure I stuck to my schooling. I got my letters and ciphers both,' he added with a touch of pride.

For men worn out from a long day's travelling and Indian fighting, there wasn't much more to be said, and so the conversation tailed off. The absence of any artificial light also encouraged them to turn in. The next day would see them crossing yet another river, the Colorado, before eventually arriving at the fort, which for Woodrow Clayton and Jared Tucker would likely be only the true beginning of their gruelling odyssey. If the latter had been privy to both the location and parlous condition of his young daughter, he would likely have stolen Clayton's horse and set off there and then, with no thought of the need for sleep!

*

Strangely enough, it was the noise of barking dogs that penetrated the blanket of misery that had enveloped her for that entire day of constant movement. Although Lucy didn't immediately realize it, the canine sounds indicated that the warriors had finally returned to their village. The war party's sudden arrival in the gathering dusk was greeted by cries of joy, mingled with wailing unhappiness from the relatives of those individuals killed by Jared Tucker. That in particular did not bode well for the continued survival of his daughter.

As the mostly jubilant Comanches dismounted, Lucy's bonds were severed for the final time. Then, very curiously, probing fingers wandered over her body for a while, before she was abruptly released. Toppling helplessly from the pony, she lay in the dust praying to be left alone. Her misshapen nose throbbed continuously, but had at least stopped bleeding. Although it was beginning to get dark, many cooking fires were burning, indicating that there was no longer any fear of discovery. With the flickering light that they emitted, she was able to peer cautiously around. Beyond the village there were only shadows, but all about her tepees loomed. Constructed from slender poles and buffalo hides, the shelter that they offered actually seemed appealing to the abused young girl. Sadly, she was not yet about to inhabit any of them.

To Lucy's absolute horror, those women in mourning were no longer merely crying and gesticulating. They had produced knives and were now indulging in self-mutilation. The squaws, young and old, slashed their arms and breasts. Then one of them uttered a tremendous howl and cleanly sliced off the little finger of her left hand in one deft movement. Despite her own suffering, the young girl was transfixed by the dreadful sight. Yet far worse was to follow.

As the warriors related their stories, many eyes turned towards Lucy Tucker. As the only prisoner taken on the raid, anyone with a grievance had only her to pick on. And one particular anguished mother intended to do just that. A wizened crone of a woman, bleeding from two cuts on her left arm, stalked over to the nearest fire and extracted a burning stick.

Lucy abruptly forgot all her aches and pains. Now her attention was focused solely on the flaming object. With a massive effort, she overcame numbness and fatigue and staggered to her feet. 'You leave me be!' she cried. It had been intended as a shrill warning, but only came out as a hoarse croak.

Spitting venom, and watched with keen interest by the rest of the tribe, the aggrieved woman lunged at Lucy. The flaming brand jabbed painfully into her left shoulder, scorching the grubby cotton dress. The young girl screamed, but instead of backing away she did something totally unexpected. The pent-up anger and grief at the slaughter of her mother and brother suddenly boiled over, and she lashed out with all of her limited strength. As her right fist struck the Comanche's face, the woman jerked back in surprise.

'You killed my ma!' Lucy wailed at no one in partic-ular. She couldn't even recall who had committed the foul act. All she did know was that her beloved mother was dead.

For a long moment, the lone white girl stood in the centre of the village with her little fist clenched, as though challenging the entire tribe. Then the inevitable happened. The startled squaw, toughened by years of toil on the plains, recovered and lashed out repeatedly with the blazing stick. It struck Lucy on the face and neck, burning her young flesh. Screaming, she staggered back, stumbled and fell. Tossing the stick aside, her tormentor spat at her and then drew a skinning knife from her waistband. Both terrified and mesmerised by the wickedly honed blade, Lucy could only watch helplessly as its point dived towards her.

A grip like iron suddenly closed over the woman's wrist, stopping her in her tracks. Then, following a sharp tug, she found herself facing the young warrior who had originally kidnapped the diminutive Texan. He shook his head, and apparently uttered some form of rebuke. The old squaw scowled at him, but had no choice other than to slink away, back to her very public display of grief. Glancing at his trembling prisoner, the Comanche gestured for her to follow him. Secure in the knowledge that she would do so, he turned away towards a tepee. Had Lucy been older and wiser, it might have occurred to her to wonder just what she had been rescued for. As it was, she meekly got to her feet and followed her dubious saviour.

Fort Concho, unsurprisingly located on the North Concho river, was a welcome sight for the weary, travel-stained freighters. Its reassuring presence meant hot food and safety, both of which had lately been in short supply. The miles of empty, open plains that surrounded the collection of buildings only seemed to emphasize the sheer loneliness of the frontier. Home to the Fourth Cavalry, the fort was relatively well built compared to most US Army posts. A continuous work in progress, due to the shortage of labour, it was being constructed out of sandstone by civilian contractors, who were also utilizing exceptionally hard Pecan wood for the beams and rafters. The lack of an enclosing stockade might have surprised some visitors, but in truth there was little need for one. No Comanches had ever been known to directly assault an army garrison.

As the freight wagons rattled their way towards the grain store, the two men accompanying them gazed about at the large parade ground and the various structures surrounding it, until they spotted the one they required. They also witnessed something else that took them by surprise, bearing in mind that they were on government property. A swarthy, fleshy individual had been stripped to the waist and spread-eagled across a horizontal wagon wheel. Tightly bound, and in the full glare of the sun, he appeared to be in a bad way.

Noting their interest, Giddings remarked. 'Don't pay that fella no mind. Doubtless he deserves it, and the colonel ain't always too particular over how he extracts information from prisoners.'

Clayton tied his mount to a hitching rail outside the

49

stables before joining his companion. Tucker had
endured a bone-shaking ride, high up on a bench
seat, and so very gratefully dropped down to join him.
They received cheerful farewells from the freighters,
but somehow both men intuitively sensed that they
hadn't seen the last of them.

'I reckon that's the best place to start,' Tucker
remarked, indicating the large headquarters building
over near the parade ground. It occurred to him that
they might just have arrived at a providential time,
because as the two of them headed over to it, they had
to keep stopping and starting to avoid all the foot
traffic. The tremendous hive of activity around them
indicated that something out of the ordinary was definitely in the offing.

'We need to see the colonel,' Clayton peremptorily
announced, before the door had even closed behind
them.

The grizzled veteran manning the desk in the small
and otherwise empty room surely possessed more
yellow stripes on his sleeves than any man had a right
to, and appeared singularly unimpressed by the
request. After slowly looking the newcomers up and
down, he remarked, 'Is that a God-damn fact? And just
who the hell might you be?'

To his credit, Clayton held his ground. 'I'm a
buffalo hunter. I've come all the way from Adobe
Walls, up on the Canadian, to warn your commanding
officer about the Comanche threat.'

The non-com rearranged a wad of chewing tobacco
in his mouth before responding. 'Well, that's right

neighbourly of you, mister, but I don't reckon there's a man on this post that hasn't realized by now that them bastard Comanches pose a threat. I also don't need telling where Adobe Walls is. So if you'll just be moving on, I'd be much obliged.'

Jared Tucker had heard more than enough. With his nerves permanently on edge and his heart pumping fit to burst, there was only one thing on his mind. Sharply rapping the muzzle of his Winchester on the sergeant major's desk, he barked out, 'I don't have time for this shit. My daughter has been taken by savages, and one way or another I aim to find her. I've served my time in your army, so the least you could do is help me!'

His last words had risen to the level of a bellow, audible far beyond that room. For a few moments there was relative silence, as the former soldier locked stares with the apparently unhelpful regular. Then a door at the end of the room swung open, and an erect figure strode into view. All three men turned to look at him.

'What part of "I'm not to be disturbed" didn't you understand, sergeant major?' he snapped out.

Before the abruptly flustered non-com could fashion a response, Tucker replied. 'The two of us have come an awful long way to ask for your help, Colonel. And we've seen a great many things that should be of interest to you. So the least you can do is hear us out.'

For a few seconds, the commanding officer fixed his chill gaze on them. Then he sharply jerked his head. 'Follow me.'

Pleasantly surprised, the two visitors trooped after him into a large but sparsely furnished office. As the full 'bird' colonel stepped behind his desk, the civilians took the opportunity to observe him. And he certainly made interesting viewing. Ranald Slidell Mackenzie was of medium height and slim, with, for the time, short fair hair. His age was hard to determine. The brutality of combat and the responsibilities of office were etched deeply into features that might otherwise have been youthful. Although unfashionably clean shaven, he did sport a set of long sideburns, named after a fellow Civil War general called Burnside. His blue uniform was immaculate, and he possessed an indefinable presence that seemed to fill the room. It was only as he turned to face them that they both noticed his deformed right hand, with two fingers completely missing. He showed scant reaction to their scrutiny, and wasted no time on niceties.

'Who are you?' he sharply demanded, all the while favouring the former soldier with an intense gaze.

'Jared Tucker.'

'And what brings you to Fort Concho, Mister Tucker?'

'Comanches killed my wife and son, and carried off my daughter from our homestead on the Red.'

'And where were you when this was happening?'

'Trying to stay alive. Because without me she's lost!'

Mackenzie digested that for a moment, before switching his attention. 'And you?'

Clayton briefly, but graphically, described the

bloody siege near the Canadian, the things that he had witnessed since, and the reason for his long ride south.

A slight rising of the eyebrows was the colonel's only visible response. 'So you're a hide hunter with a conscience. That's a novelty, to be sure.'

Clayton shook his head in disbelief at the display of cynicism. 'You can think of me how you will, Colonel, but I hear tell that some of your generals quite approve of folks like me killing the Indians' food source. And the fact that I'm here, rather than shooting buffalo for profit, kind of proves my intentions. I sure ain't got any other bona fides to show you.'

'Except that on my oath, I can back up some of what he's told you,' Tucker stated. 'And we did help to save your supply wagons when they were attacked. That ought to count for something.'

Mackenzie slowly eased into his chair, wincing slightly as he finally got settled. For a man possibly only in his early thirties, he did not appear to be in the best of health. For long moments he seemed to stare right through them, apparently lost in thought. Finally he sighed, and his features softened slightly.

'Very well, gentlemen. I am prepared to accept that you have both come to me in good faith. And although I was naturally unaware of the particular events that you have described, they come as no surprise to me. Because sadly, the slaughtering of settlers and taking of children is nothing new in this harsh land. What is new is that President Grant has abandoned his peace policy, and has placed all Indian agencies under military control. For the first time the army is authorized to employ whatever force is necessary. I am under orders from General Sheridan to once and for all bring an end to these dreadful depredations. To that end, my intention is to lead a punitive expedition up on to the Llano Estacado to seek out Quanah Parker's Quahadi Comanches. They are without doubt the worst of the holdouts. It is my belief that if I can break them, then the others will accept the inevitable, and move on to the reservation near Fort Sill.'

Tucker nodded intently. 'Then one way or another I'm going along too. Either with you, or trailing along behind. Because if Lucy is out there on this Llano Estacado, I intend to find her, or die trying.'

'And if you do find her, what then?'

The settler was nonplussed in relation to the unexpected question.

The colonel sighed irritably. 'Is it your intention to try and buy her freedom? Such things have been done in the past.'

Tucker's expression noticeably chilled. 'The thought of paying those same bastards that killed my wife and son doesn't sit well with me.'

Mackenzie's eyes narrowed slightly. 'Nevertheless, it is something you should give consideration to if you get the opportunity. Because remember, I am going up there to pick a fight! Everything else is secondary.' Without waiting for a reply, he then favoured Clayton with a hard glance. 'And I suppose you mean to go along with him, being as how you've sworn off hunting for a while?'

That man smiled slightly and nodded. 'Where he goes, I go. At least until this business is settled.'

'Very commendable, I'm sure,' the officer dryly remarked, before abruptly getting to his feet. The interview was obviously about to be curtailed, but not in the way that they had been beginning to expect. 'I am undoubtedly a hard taskmaster, but I am also fair. If the army is indeed indebted to you for helping bring in the supplies, then I will allow you to accompany the column. Because, gentlemen, if there's one thing I've learned in my career, it is to utilize every available asset. I will also ensure that you are compensated for all cartridges used assisting my forces, but you will, of course, be subject to military discipline at all times. You step out of line with me, and you'll wish that the Comanches had captured you! We leave at first light. Dismissed!'

Back in the outer office, the two men stood in contemplative silence for a moment, before glancing over at the sergeant major. 'Is he always like that?' Clayton queried.

The other man grinned, but kept his voice low. 'He can be a mite prickly at times, but I reckon on how he's got good reason. There's a powerful lot to be done out here, and it's all on his shoulders.' He paused for a moment before proving that he had overheard all or most of their meeting with his commander. 'Anyhoo, since you two fellas are coming with us, you'd better haul your possibles into the stables. Tell Sergeant Mulroney that I said he's to see you and your animals fed and watered.'

'Mine was killed by a Comanche,' Tucker stated.

The non-com grunted. 'It was, huh? Well, one thing the Fourth ain't short of right now is remounts. Mind you, that might not be the case once Quanah Parker's warriors have had a crack at us.'

Tucker nodded. 'Much obliged to you, sergeant major.'

As the two men turned to leave, that individual did have one last thing to impart. With his craggy features suddenly hard, the menace in his voice was unmistakable. 'Oh, and if you ever point that Winchester at me again, you'd better be sure an' use it!'

CHAPTER FIVE

The ease and efficiency with which the entire column came together was truly astonishing. At first light, five hundred and sixty enlisted men, forty-seven officers, and three surgeons belonging to seven companies of the Fourth Cavalry Regiment mustered on the parade ground in columns of four abreast. They were joined by thirty-two Tonkawa scouts, eager, as always, to shed Comanche blood. Not until they were all assembled did their commander appear from the headquarters building. Mackenzie carefully scrutinized them in silence for a few moments, before striding to the fore. Here he stiffly mounted a waiting horse, and still without a word moved off onto the trackless plains heading north.

'He's a cool one, an' no mistake,' muttered Woodrow Clayton. 'I suppose we're expected to follow on in their dust.'

'I don't care what he's like, so long as he can find and fight Comanches,' Jared Tucker irritably retorted.

His features were drawn from lack of sleep. Not unnaturally, he had passed an unsettled night in the stables, agonizing over his daughter's likely condition. Deep down, he was no longer completely convinced that accompanying a military expedition was the best way to rescue Lucy safely.

Unlike many other martial send-offs, particularly those under the control of a certain Lieutenant Colonel George Armstrong Custer, there were no bands, bugles or fanfare of any kind. The men just simply followed their prematurely aged colonel off the post. Every man involved had a fair idea of what awaited him, and in most cases they were up for it.

As they urged their animals into motion, Tucker peered grimly over at the Tonkawas. His limited and decidedly poor experience of Indians meant that he now viewed them all with grave suspicion.

'I'll tell you this much,' he muttered darkly. 'If one of those sons-of-bitches points a firearm anywhere near me, I'll blow his Goddamn head off!'

Clayton nodded understandingly, but nevertheless attempted to calm his companion's simmering hatred. 'I don't think the colonel would much like you killing his scouts. From what I hear, it's only on account of them that the army's even able to track hostile Indians.' Pausing, he tried to choose his next words carefully. 'So it could be the case that those sons-of-bitches are your best chance of finding Lucy alive.'

Tucker twisted towards him with a face like thunder, and for an instant Clayton feared that he'd gone too far. Then the other man blinked rapidly, as though emerging from a particularly chilling daydream, and his 'head of steam' abruptly diminished. 'Yeah, well, happen you could be right,' he reluctantly acknowledged, before quickly adding, 'But that don't mean I have to trust them.'

Fort Concho was barely out of sight before the column encountered a broad trail, rutted and worn from countless years of use. Some of the veterans crossed themselves, and with good reason. This was part of the infamous 'Comanche Trace', one of a number of routes used by war parties on their way to and from Mexico. For those poor wretches abducted and forcibly transported on the return trip, it was surely the road to abject misery. It was no coincidence that the fort had been situated in such close proximity to it.

For the first few miles the two men rode in silence, each occupied by his own thoughts. They had pulled off to one side of the long column to avoid the choking dust created by a long spell of hot, dry weather. So it was that they were able to spot the officer riding back to join them. As he drew closer, the captain's bars on his shoulders became visible.

'You can only be the two fellas that the colonel agreed could tag along,' he remarked amiably. 'You sure must have impressed him, because normally any unknown civilians would be sent packing.'

'I reckon helping the freighters keep their scalps had a lot to do with it,' Clayton replied. 'Or maybe we just appealed to his good nature.'

That brought a broad smile to the captain's tanned features. 'Ahah, well, I wouldn't mention that around the enlisted men. Most of them don't believe that their commanding officer is even human. But I've served with Colonel Mackenzie for years, and one thing I can swear to is that he is always a fair man.' He paused, as though recollecting something. 'My name's Beaumont, by the way. Eugene Beaumont.'

The two civilians introduced themselves amicably enough, but Jared Tucker quickly demonstrated that he was a man on a mission. 'In case you don't know it, captain, my daughter was taken by Comanches a few days ago. Your colonel can be a fire-breathing dragon for all I care, just so long as he can do his job.'

Beaumont regarded him calmly. 'Ulysses S. Grant once said that Mackenzie was the most promising young officer in the whole army, and I'd stand by that. And let me explain something to you.

Traditionally, the US Army has spent a lot of its time riding the plains and not finding any hostiles. Faced with as many men as we've got, they'd just vanish, and even the Tonks would struggle to cut their trail. But that won't happen with Quanah's warriors. Thanks to the talkative Comanchero that you'll have seen yesterday clinging to the wagon wheel, Mackenzie has a fair notion of where we're headed, and then they will find us for sure. But here's the rub. There's lots of different bands of hostiles out there. If she's still alive, your girl could be anywhere. You could spend months out here, and never catch a glimpse.'

Tucker stared at him fixedly for a moment. The

60

thought that his little girl might already be dead was almost too much to endure. Then something suddenly occurred to him. 'The leader of those that took her wore a buffalo scalp and horns.'

The soldier pondered for a moment. 'That means nothing to me, but I'll talk with the scouts.' He glanced over at the column. 'I have duties to perform. We'll speak on this matter again.' With that, he courteously touched his campaign hat and wheeled his horse away.

Tucker could feel frustration nibbling at his guts, but there was simply nothing more that he could do for the present. He did, however, retain enough awareness to realize that he should say something to his tolerant companion. Turning to Clayton, he said, 'Don't pay me no mind if I act like a bear with a sore head. Only this not knowing is eating me up inside.'

After travelling all day without any let-up, and ending with the cavalry and its attendants safely crossing the Clear Fork of the Brazos without incident, the whole force finally made camp on the bone-dry terrain to the north of it. The following day would hopefully see them in the shelter of Blanco Canyon, used in the past as a supply base.

Mackenzie's Tonkawa scouts had not brought any news of Comanche activity, but he was taking no chances. All the animals were hobbled, and then their forelegs were tied to opposite hind legs, a procedure known as cross sidelining. Then they were roped to iron stakes driven deep into the ground. In addition, he posted groups of troopers known as 'sleeping parties' around the horse herd. On previous expeditions in West Texas, the Fourth had suffered the loss of many horses to the hostiles, but this time it would be different. Yet sadly, there was one element that the colonel could not guard against.

With their supply wagons forming a partial stockade, the drivers had gathered around a campfire of their own. As Clayton and Tucker approached it in search of a fire to cook their vittles, they recognized a familiar face.

'I kind of thought we might run across you again,' Clayton remarked quietly.

Josiah Giddings beamed up at them. 'The colonel was short of drivers for this trip, which meant higher wages. Sit yourselves down. You're among friends here, not a bunch of slack-jawed soldier boys. No offence intended,' he jovially called over to the nearest bemused troopers.

The two men willingly joined them, but it was left to Clayton to make the conversation. During the long gruelling ride under the relentless sun, Tucker had withdrawn into himself to a dark place from which he hadn't yet emerged. Even after consuming a plateful of beans and bacon, he was only able to manage a few grunts. But then the weather took a hand, and literally everything changed.

From out of nowhere came a howling 'norther' that swept through the large encampment, turning the benign cooking fires into minor infernos. The relative tranquillity they had all been enjoying vanished in seconds, as soldiers and civilians alike struggled to control belongings and equipment. Then the violent wind demonstrated just how dangerous it could be. Sparks from the energized fires leapt out across the desiccated grass, sparking numerous conflagrations.

As the entire command abruptly recognized the danger, they desperately attempted to extinguish the campfires without the need for any orders from their officers. And yet it was a case of too little too late. The damage had already been done, because by then, driven by the overwhelming power of nature, all the individual prairie fires were linking up with awesome speed to form a huge firestorm. The only thing that saved the men and animals was the fact that the 'norther' blew north to south, ensuring that the flames spread away from the Fourth. With the river only a short distance away, the terrifying blaze would shortly burn itself out. But of course, the damage had already been done.

Jared Tucker stared up at the night sky, now glowing with a frightening intensity, and uttered his first full sentence since noon. 'Well, if those heathen savages didn't already know we were coming, they sure as hell do now!'

Quanah Parker absentmindedly patted the partially healed wound between his neck and shoulder blade. During the Adobe Walls siege, a bullet had ricocheted off the powder horn that he habitually carried around his neck, and had then lodged itself painfully in his flesh. The misshapen lead had subsequently been removed, leaving a shallow gash that was not serious. But every now and then it would remind him of its irritating presence, and also of an encounter with the cursed hide hunters that he would rather forget.

Unusually for a Plains Indian, Quanah was exceptionally tall and strongly built. But of course that was explained by the fact that he was also of white Texan stock, son of the kidnapped Cynthia Ann Parker who had eventually married Peta Nocona, a Comanche chief. Although only about thirty, Quanah, now a war chief of the Quahadi band, had already won considerable renown as the most capable leader within the dwindling Comanche nation. Yet the unexpected reverse at Adobe Walls meant that a victory was urgently required to maintain the fighting spirit of his suffering people. And now it appeared that he would get the chance to lead his warriors against the equally famous 'Bad Hand' Mackenzie. Word had been brought to him that a large number of 'horse soldiers' were making for his fastness in the Llano Estacado.

This vast area of inhospitable land eventually spread west into what the Americanos had taken to calling New Mexico Territory. Part of what was once known as the Great American Desert, it had in the previous century been absorbed into Comancheria, the great Comanche stronghold. These 'horse Indians' had discovered the various canyons and water sources that made life there possible. It was also referred to with somewhat sinister significance as the Staked Plains, and for those unused to its desolate waste, it remained a frightening place to venture into.

Smiling, Quanah remarked that it was very gener-
ous of the white soldiers to present so many animals to
him as a gift. Whoops of delight from his assembled
warriors greeted that apt witticism. They all remembered the last time the bluecoats had entered their
domain, and how easy it had been to run their mounts
off. It didn't occur to them that this time it might all
be very different!

After the fraught events of the previous night, the
long column had broken camp at first light. Now travelling in a north-westerly direction, it had to battle a
strong residual wind, but otherwise made good time
for the whole of that day without encountering any
hostiles. It was close to nightfall when the entire body
of men entered the mouth of the canyon.

Back in the mists of time, Blanco Canyon had been
eroded out of the caprock escarpment on the east side
of the Llano Estacado. It now provided an ideal refuge
from the weather's extremes, but not from the
Comanches. At thirty-four miles long and up to ten
miles across, it was impossible for the soldiers to
prevent incursions by the fast-moving Indians. Which
turned out to be the reason behind an unexpected
summons for Woodrow Clayton to attend Colonel
Mackenzie in his tent.

'Mister Clayton. After last night's mishap, I fully
expect that our camp will be attacked tonight in force.
The Comanches will seek to deprive us of our horses.
I know this because it has happened before. On that
occasion it succeeded, but this time it will not.' The

colonel stood stiffly, as though in some degree of pain, all the while rubbing the stumps of his severed fingers. The flickering light from a kerosene lamp illuminated the commanding officer's tent. 'You may wonder what this has to do with you, but as I said before, I intend to utilize every available asset. As a buffalo hunter, I would imagine you are a fine shot, and therefore well able to help defend the horse herd.'

Despite the officer's reserve, Clayton favoured him with a broad smile. 'It would be my pleasure, colonel. An' how about Jared Tucker? He's a fair hand with his Winchester, and a mite faster than your troopers with their Spencers and "trapdoor" Springfields.'

Mackenzie curtly nodded his agreement, and then called out to someone waiting beyond the tent's flap. The brief interview was apparently over, and the hunter turned to leave.

'Does your friend realize that his child may well be dead by now?'

Startled, Clayton glanced over at the soldier and found himself staring into intense, almost feverish eyes. He thought for a moment. 'Your Captain Beaumont mentioned the possibility, but I don't believe that Jared can accept it,' he finally replied.

'Well then, you should watch yourself around him. Because if he does, he'll be a dangerous man to be around. Thank you, Mister Clayton.' This time their meeting was definitely over.

The two men sat on the grass in silence. The hobbled and securely fastened horse herd grazed behind them.

To either side but some distance away, troopers lay in the grass, occasionally talking softly. With only a new moon providing illumination, overall visibility was poor. Darkness held the cold camp in its grip. Shadows from the canyon's walls mingled with those in men's imagination. There was an indefinable tension in the air that was felt by everyone. In other, less disciplined commands, such conditions would have resulted in itchy trigger fingers, but Mackenzie had subjected his men to relentless training. They only fired at flesh and blood, or would surely answer to him!

With the lack of activity, Tucker's thoughts had wandered. He was away with Lucy in a world of gruesome possibilities. Thus it was Clayton who first spotted movement where there shouldn't have been any. A great dark, seething mass had swept into the canyon at speed. Yet before he could say anything, an alert horse herd guard bellowed out, 'Hostiles! Stand to!'

As all around them troopers scrambled into position and cocked their weapons, Clayton demanded, 'You back with me, Jared?'

'Oh yeah,' came the definite response.

The ground seemed to shake as the thundering phalanx drew closer. The Comanches were heading directly for the horses, and suddenly unleashed a cacophony of sound. Howling and screaming, it was obvious what their intentions were. Clayton was first to fire, and his 'truthful' Sharps didn't let him down. The heavy bullet threw a warrior off the back of his pony, and under the hooves of those following. Even as he

67

reloaded, Tucker and the soldiers around them opened up. The homesteader's heart was filled with pure malice, and he worked the lever-action with machine-like efficiency. The soldiers couldn't hope to match his rate of fire, but between them managed to throw plenty of hot lead at the fast approaching Indians. Nevertheless, there weren't yet enough defenders to deflect the charge.

The whooping savages swept into the tethered horse herd, but to their surprise and dismay were unable to run off any of them. Whinnying with fear, the army mounts bucked and tugged, but were simply too well secured. Swinging away in some confusion, the Comanches continued on into the main camp, but their momentum had slowed, and now they were faced with tents and heavy wagons.

Mackenzie appeared outside his tent, the oil lamp having been hastily extinguished. 'Hold fire!' he commanded, in a voice that could have cut through ice. He well realized that, with the enemy in their midst, his troopers were as much a danger to each other as they were to the Indians.

The Comanches could and should have caused havoc, but instead displayed one of their fatal flaws. Born to the open plains, they had an inherent fear of enclosed spaces. Hemmed in by wagons, tents and the infuriatingly immovable horse herd, exhilaration turned to anxiety. The desire to attack rapidly became a need to retreat. And so they extricated themselves with extraordinary speed, but in doing so became targets again.

'Open fire!' Mackenzie now bellowed, and his order was taken up by officers and non-coms throughout the camp. Individual gunshots were no longer distinguishable as hundreds of men willingly complied. Vast numbers of muzzle flashes lit up the night, like a deadly firework display.

As Jared Tucker watched the inevitable retreat, a kind of madness overcame him. Those heathen savages had slaughtered his wife and son, and kidnapped his lovely daughter. Although he hadn't yet found Lucy, he could sure as hell make them pay! Leaping to his feet, the solitary avenger ran after the fleeing Indians, wildly firing his Winchester.

Woodrow Clayton couldn't believe his eyes. 'Sweet Jesus, Jared, get down,' he yelled.

Overcome with bloodlust, Tucker was oblivious to everything except attempting to kill Comanches. Empty cartridge cases flew up from the breech until the inevitable happened. His rifle dry-fired. And then, rather than come to his senses and retire, he merely stood there, apparently dumbfounded. Those soldiers nearest to him, having realized that he was white, aimed elsewhere. So it was that he found himself alone and unsupported . . . except for the hide hunter.

Some sixth sense alerted one of the retreating Comanches to the chance of an easy kill. Wheeling his pony around with the skill of a natural predator, the warrior hefted his lance in one hand. For a mere split second, he weighed his chances and then dug his heels in. Pony and rider were as one, as they pounded towards Jared Tucker's strangely inanimate figure. Even the terrifying sight of the lance aimed directly at him failed to generate a response.

After shaking his head in disbelief, Clayton took rapid aim at the larger target and squeezed off his shot. The pony's front legs buckled under the savage impact, sending the Comanche flying over its head. Unfortunately for Tucker, there was no broken neck to slow him down. With startling agility, the warrior rolled twice before coming to a halt on his feet. Only then did Tucker finally begin to react, but rather than draw his holster gun, he bizarrely chose to use his empty Winchester as a club. Perhaps he wanted to feel his victim's pain.

The Comanche must have realized that being on foot so close to the soldier camp meant that his death was certain, but he didn't hesitate for a second. Even as his opponent's gun butt streaked towards him, the Indian unslung a bow from over his shoulder. Then, suddenly ducking down, he viciously swung it in a wide arc. Tucker missed his strike, and so was already off balance as the bow hit him behind the right knee. The force was sufficient to send him tumbling back to the hard ground, dropping his rifle in the process. Only then did he attempt to draw his revolver.

Knowing that he couldn't bring a knife to a gun-fight, the warrior did the only thing possible. Frenziedly lashing out with the bow, he repeatedly struck Tucker about his body, who could only attempt to shield himself from the painful blows.

Clayton had by now reloaded his Sharps and moved

in closer. The mounted Comanches were no longer a threat, and so he paused, strangely in no all-fired hurry to shoot the lone and undoubtedly brave warrior. Watching his companion being soundly thrashed, a faint smile began to lift the edges of his mouth.

As Tucker twisted about like an eel, desperately trying to avoid the vigorous clouts, he suddenly caught sight of Clayton, motionless in the gloom. 'Shoot him, for Christ's sake!' he breathlessly demanded.

As some of the horse-herd guard curiously wandered over to join him, Clayton remarked, 'Save your powder, boys. This one's mine . . . soon.'

Deciding that there was some entertainment to be had, the troopers merely shrugged their agreement. Bemusement turned to laughter, and they began to make raucous comments, and yell suggestions. The desperate Comanche knew very well what was to come, and so determined to at least take one of the hated Texans with him. Retaining the bow in only one hand, he reached for his knife. With the fallen white man still reeling under the blows and unable to defend himself, all he needed to do was get in one good thrust.

Clayton missed the furtive movement, but saw moonlight glint on the honed blade. The time had surely come to end this unpleasant spectacle. Raising the Sharps to his shoulder, he swiftly drew a bead on the doomed warrior. Recognizing his fate, that individual unleashed a banshee wail of defiance just before the hammer fell. With all other firing now finished, the single shot crashed out in the night. A large bullet tore into the Comanche's bare chest with enough force to kill a buffalo at a thousand yards, snuffing out his life in an instant. His body had barely hit the ground before the recriminations began.

'You God-damn son-of-a-bitch,' Tucker breathlessly exclaimed. 'He near beat me to a pulp.'

The watching soldiers turned away chuckling. The show was over, and they were suddenly alert for the scrutiny of their fearsome commanding officer.

Clayton walked over to help his companion to his feet, but that man angrily waved him away. 'What the hell was all that about?' he shouted. 'Why take so long to kill him?'

Not until he had replaced the spent cartridge did Clayton favour him with an answer. 'Someone needed to beat a little sense into you! Who better to do it than one of those tarnal cockchafers?'

CHAPTER SIX

Dawn arrived, and with it came a strange stillness in the air that seemed to reflect the mood throughout the camp. Even though the marauders had apparently fled after the failed attack, the soldiers of the Fourth had mostly been too edgy to get much shuteye. Now, as they gazed anxiously over at the mouth of Blanco Canyon, they mainly pondered in silence over just what perils the new day might hold.

Jared Tucker was one of the few men with no immediate interest in what the sunrise might bring. He had passed the sleepless night engrossed in a form of exquisite self-torture, as he mentally explored every possible horrific scenario relating to his absent daughter. Personal guilt played a large role in his tormented imaginings, for he cursed himself for indulging in the solitary, and in truth unnecessary excursion beyond the frontier. And yet, something positive had finally come from it all. As he collected up his bedroll, he glanced searchingly over at his companion.

'You were right to let that savage beat on me,' he

73

softly opined. 'I acted like an addle-brained fool. I'm no use to Lucy dead, an' I could have got other folks kilt as well.'

'That's what I figured,' Clayton responded. 'And so did the colonel. That man sure don't miss much!'

Tucker sighed. 'What I'm trying to say is, it won't happen again. On my oath, you can rely on me from here on in.'

'Well, good for you,' came the sharp, somewhat sarcastic retort.

Feeling that his apology was being treated dismissively, Tucker was beginning to get annoyed. 'You got some real hard bark on you, Woody!'

'Maybe so,' that man replied. 'But if we're gonna stay alive out here, and get your daughter back, then we both of us need to stay sharp. Yeah?'

Tucker stared at him long and hard, before a smile finally spread over his careworn features. 'Yeah!'

Lucy Tucker's new life seemed to consist of unending toil, labouring from dawn 'til dusk with no respite, and occasionally interspersed with moments of paralysing fear. And then there were the nights, spent with what could only be described as her new owner, the young warrior who had originally carried her off. Strange things took place that left her numb and trembling, until finally she quietly cried herself to sleep thinking of her family. Her broken nose was no longer as painful, but cautious exploration of it revealed that it was definitely misshapen.

The Comanche village, her new home, was located

in a massively walled canyon, with lush grass, lots of trees for shade, and a creek flowing through it. She had no idea where it was in relation to the Tucker homestead, but even to her jaundiced mind it was an undeniably attractive location. Protected by such a high enclosure, she could visualize just how sheltered it would be in winter. And there was ample space to accommodate the vast pony herd, which made all Comanches the envy of the other Southern Plains tribes.

A sharp pain flared on her right thigh, effectively rebuking the young girl for daydreaming. One of the many lined old women in the village had lashed out at her with a rawhide whip. Sometimes there seemed to be no reason for such treatment other than sadistic pleasure. Blinking back the tears, she continued scratching away at the large buffalo hide pegged out on the ground. It was her task to remove every scrap of dried flesh from the inside of it. Even when her fingers bled from the gruelling work, there was still no relief.

Waiting until the crone's attention wandered, she then surreptitiously stole a glance towards one end of the huge canyon. There was a perilously steep path leading up and out of it. If only she could steal a pony and get to the rim. But although she had seen warriors ride up and down it with apparent ease, she was very doubtful of her chances, especially in the dark. And even if she did make it, where would she go afterwards? She had no idea of the direction to take. Fresh tears came to her eyes. Why couldn't her pa come for her, like he had promised he would?

Again the knotted whip flicked out at her thigh, and this time the old woman snarled something at her. Lucy bit her lip, and renewed her efforts. Anger replaced distress, as the girl thought of all the things she would like to do to her tormentor. Had she been much older, it might have occurred to her that deliberately nurturing such feelings were her best hope of staying alive!

Colonel Ranald Mackenzie surveyed the Comanche horde with gritted teeth and through narrowed eyes. Many of the watching troopers might have attributed that to the harsh light, but those officers who knew him of old would have realized such actions were more likely due to pain. Because unfortunately, the colonel was never entirely free of it. During the late war, his almost foolhardy bravery had resulted in him being wounded six times. Since then, long periods in the saddle pursuing Indians in all weathers meant that he was almost always in constant torment. Yet none of this detracted from his efficiency. And right now he had a decision to make.

The hostiles were spread out beyond Blanco Canyon on high, level ground. Since they were quite deliberately blocking his advance, there was no easy way to avoid them, and neither would he have wished to. Unlike some officers in the service, Mackenzie had no fear of direct action. Then again, he also didn't believe in taking unnecessary casualties.

'Captain Beaumont,' he shouted. 'Be so good as to

send that hide hunter to me.'

Surprisingly, that officer chose to run the errand himself. 'I reckon the colonel has need of your Sharps, Mister Clayton.'

Together they rode over to the commanding officer at the head of the column. As ever, that man came directly to the point. 'Could you drop one of those hostiles from here with that rifle?'

Having expected such a question, Clayton had his answer ready. The distance was about half a mile, and he was no Billy Dixon, but then again the Sharps rifle was a weapon of uncommon accuracy. 'Maybe not a rider, but certainly one of the ponies. What have you got in mind, colonel?'

Mackenzie shifted in his saddle, and grimaced. 'I believe they seek to intimidate us, Mister Clayton. Or even to draw some of us into a trap. It wouldn't be the first time. So I intend that we work on their superstitious nature to turn the tables.' Awkwardly twisting to face Beaumont, he continued. 'You will form your company into line. The instant that he takes his shot, you will charge those Comanches. They're on higher ground, so initially I will, if necessary, provide covering fire for effect over your heads. Any questions?'

The veteran officer merely shook his head and saluted. He knew full well that should he need support, it would be forthcoming: something that Major Joel Elliott had found sadly lacking from Custer on the Washita some years earlier.

'Let's be about it then,' Mackenzie snapped irritably. 'We're burning daylight.'

'Don't take offence when he gets a mite testy,' Beaumont quietly remarked as they moved off. 'His old wounds trouble him something terrible. I've known him keep riding doubled over in pain.'

'You really like him, don't you?' Clayton observed.

The captain grunted. 'Like is not a word I would use for a man such as him, but I respect him a great deal . . . and he sure can soldier!'

Whilst Beaumont made his dispositions, Clayton rejoined Tucker and dismounted.

'Huh, seems like you and that rifle are right popular,' the homesteader muttered sourly.

Clayton raised the ladder sight before glancing at him. 'There's no call to get wrathy, Jared. I got a skill that happens to be useful right now, is all. You'll get your chance.' With that, he began his adjustments to compensate for the extreme distance.

Unusually for the Comanches, they had remained stationary, as though content to see how the horse soldiers would react. Quanah Parker knew all too well the destructive power of massed soldiery. If well led, no amount of manic assaults would break them. And if 'Bad Hand' was in command, then they would be! It therefore suited him to keep his impatient warriors far out of range and to wait on events.

He watched with interest as one party of 'horse soldiers' deployed at the front, whilst the rest spread in line behind them. If he could just lure the smaller group away from the rest, then his warriors might be able to cut them off and destroy them. All the plains tribes had heard tell of Crazy Horse's great victory over the bluecoats many moons ago. The impetuous soldier chief Fetterman and all his men had been wiped out near the white man's Bozeman Trail. It was the stuff of legend, and every hostile tribe was keen to repeat it.

For long moments, Quanah peered at the hated foe. 'Why do they not charge?' he pondered. Anxiety flared briefly, as it suddenly occurred to him that they might have a 'gun that shoots twice', but after some intense scrutiny he began to relax. In such open ground it was simply impossible to hide something the size of a mountain howitzer, and that was the only weapon the soldiers possessed that could hurt his warriors at so great a distance.

There was a sudden flash and puff of smoke, and quite incredibly the pony next to him whinnied in pain and shock. As Quanah stared incredulously, the poor creature toppled sideways, blood pumping from its chest. Because they hadn't been moving, its rider managed to jump clear, shaken but unharmed. A ripple of dismay swept across the assembled warriors. At that precise moment a bugle blared out shrilly, and the long rank of troopers launched forward. It was time to order a few shots fired for effect before they all supposedly fled. Yet instead, the chief merely sat his pony and stared at the advancing enemy, as fragments of the Adobe Walls fight flashed through his fevered mind. Surely his warriors couldn't be up against the same men, armed with their incredible long guns.

Another single, distant shot crashed out, and

Quanah's worst fears were confirmed. One of his men screamed and clapped a hand to his right leg, broken by a heavy bullet that had actually been aimed at the creature beneath him. Unable to stop himself, the abruptly crippled warrior slid sideways off his mount.

All thoughts of subterfuge and entrapment left the war chief's head. Although ruthless and practical, he was still prey to the same primitive superstitions that affected all his warriors. That their medicine had turned against them was inescapable, and the only option left to them was flight.

After ensuring that the wounded man had been agonizingly tied to his pony, Quanah Parker signalled that they should genuinely retreat. Disheartened by the change in fortune, after a failed night attack and now this, they needed no further urging. Turning away from the fast approaching cavalry, the Comanches streamed off to the north, towards the perceived safety of the Llano Estacado.

All of the various aches and pains in her young body abruptly paled into insignificance as Lucy cautiously peered around. On her knees in the dirt as usual, she realized with a start that no one was observing her. Even the old women were distracted by the commotion in the centre of the village. Most of the young warriors, including her owner, were mounted on their ponies and milling about in excitement. Something out of the ordinary was obviously about to happen. All she could think of was, how would it affect her? Please God she might now be left alone in the dark hours, free from the strange and painful assaults on her body.

Then the war chief appeared from his hide-covered lodge, clad in the terrifyingly distinctive buffalo scalp and horns, and a great howl of acclaim went up. Instinctively she touched her deformed nose, and prayed that his glance wouldn't fall on her. But of course someone of his eminence had no interest whatsoever in a diminutive slave. Buffalo Head, as he was known to some of the white eyes, had it in mind to join forces with other Comanche and Kiowa bands, and yet again lay waste to the Texas frontier. After much ritual, the tribe's venerable shaman had announced that the omens for such a raid were good.

For a few brief moments, the chief addressed his warriors, firing them up with more talk of obtaining fresh scalps, captives and booty to trade with the New Mexican Comancheros. Then, with a great flourish, he pointed towards the path out of the canyon. Urging his animal forward, Buffalo Head swept out of the village, followed by his whooping men. Initially the riders were accompanied by barking dogs and excited children, but they soon fell by the wayside.

As Lucy stared at the departing war party, an idea suddenly came to her. With mostly only old men, women and children left in the village, there would be no better time to flee. That night, in the dark. Excitement surged through her young body, overwhelming such annoying things as doubts and practicalities. For the first time since being taken, she felt a ray of hope. If her pa couldn't come to her, then she would go to him!

A sudden explosion of pain on her calf indicated that she was no longer ignored. The rawhide whip had been wielded viciously enough to draw blood this time. Yelping in anguish, she glanced venomously at the old woman, who in turn merely grinned wolfishly at her and shook her head. She it was who had originally taken against her, and there had been no softening in attitude. The answer to childish defiance was always the same. And so it was that another stinging flick of the whip brought Lucy's attention completely back to her mind-numbing task. Yet this time there was a warm glow inside, at the prospect of finally escaping from the clutches of this horrible old crone. It didn't occur to her adolescent mind that the execution of such a bold idea might be a whole lot harder than the thinking of it!

'You did good this morning, Mister Clayton,' Captain Beaumont remarked. 'Real good! The colonel's quite taken by your skill with that rifle.'

The buffalo hunter glanced at him in the fading light and smiled. 'That's mighty kind of you, captain, but do me a favour, huh? Mister Clayton has me looking for the warrant in your hand. My friends call me Woody.'

'Fair enough, Woody.'

The column, free of any impediments, had been pushed hard all day by its impatient commander. After consulting briefly with his senior officers, Mackenzie had decided to leave the supply wagons in Blanco Canyon, along with one company as protection. The freighter, Josiah Giddings, had gleefully wished the two civilians well. Now getting paid to just sit in a canyon, he was quite obviously very content at not having to continue the tiring and dangerous pursuit.

Under the relentless burning sunlight, the Fourth Cavalry had moved up over the Caprock Escarpment that marked the limit of the plains country, and on to the thoroughly inhospitable Llano Estacado. Mile after mile of bone-hard ground stretched ahead of them, totally devoid of any trees or vegetation. Without prior knowledge of the available water sources, the troopers' survival would last only as long as the liquid in their canteens. Fortunately, Colonel Mackenzie had travelled this land before, hunting the same hostiles that he sought now. He had made his mistakes and lived to tell the tale. Now he was back to impose his iron will upon the terrain and everything in it.

Beaumont spotted Jared Tucker a few yards away, apparently deep in thought, and so lowered his voice for his next remark. 'Does your friend realize that even if, by some miracle, he gets his daughter back, she sure as hell won't be the girl she once was?'

Clayton was taken aback. For sure he'd heard stories of children being carried off by Indians, but he was a hunter, not a soldier or Texas Ranger. Until very recently, his job had purely involved the killing of dumb creatures for cash money. 'Well, we're not really friends as such,' he responded quietly. 'I just sort of came across him and stuck around. Helping him find his girl seemed like the right thing to do.'

The officer nodded understandingly. 'Very admirable I'm sure, but think on this. Those God-damned Comanches don't have any notion of civilized life. The horrors they inflict on prisoners ain't fit to be spoken about to anyone with tender sensibilities. She'll likely be broken in spirit and ruined for life. Someone that no white man would ever contemplate taking as a wife.'

'You don't paint a very pretty picture, captain. If it's as bad as you say, why do families even live out on the frontier?'

'Because there's some mighty fine land out in West Texas, and it's free for the taking . . . if you can defend it. A lot of poor folks came out here after the war to make a new start, but all that many have found is a cold hole in the ground . . . or worse. But the head honchos in Washington have finally woken up to the problem, which is why we're here.'

Before Clayton could respond, Jared Tucker rode up to join them. 'Those scouts of yours seem mighty skittish about something, captain. They're moving around like they're on hot coals. An' I'll tell you something else as well. We're not headed north any more.'

Beaumont nodded. 'The Tonks know there's Comanches out there, shadowing the column until we pitch camp. Except we ain't going to. The colonel's waiting 'til it's full dark before turning north and striking out for Palo Duro Canyon. There's a big village there that he intends to attack.'

As Tucker digested all that, his now habitually grim expression changed to one of great alarm. 'The hell you say. What if Lucy's in there, an' we all go boiling in shooting everything that moves?'

To be fair to the captain, he suddenly appeared incredibly uncomfortable, but that didn't influence his response. 'You've got to understand, Mister Tucker, that the life of one child can't be allowed to jeopardize the whole mission!'

Tucker stared at him askance. 'You sound like you're quoting from an army manual . . . or maybe a stuffed shirt in a colonel's uniform. Either way, it's high time him an' me had words.' With that, he wheeled his horse away and made straight for the head of the column.

'Oh shit!' Captain Beaumont exclaimed. 'If he's not careful, he'll end up like that Comanchero back at the fort!'

CHAPTER SEVEN

As darkness fell, the village soon grew quiet. All of the young men were on the war trail. One warrior in particular was no longer able to make unwelcome demands on his young prisoner, and if all went to plan she wouldn't be there when he returned.

Lucy Tucker lay outside her owner's lodge on a meagre bed of worn and filthy animal skins. Her heart was thumping so loudly at the prospect of escape that she felt sure everyone within earshot must hear. Tentatively glancing around, the trembling girl was amazed to find herself all alone. All she had to do was get to the pony herd without being seen. In truth, the thought of tackling the steep track in darkness still terrified her, but then so did the prospect of remaining with the Comanches.

Rising off the makeshift bed, Lucy stood still and listened. Nobody had thought to tie her up, because presumably it was thought that she would have no idea where to escape to . . . which actually wasn't far from the truth. The biggest danger she faced was discovery by any of the stray dogs that wandered the village living off food scraps. By the light of the moon, she spotted one sidling round the edge of a lodge some distance away. Other than that, she appeared to have the night to herself. Breathing a cautious sigh of relief, the bruised and bloodied captive tentatively moved off towards where the ponies were grazing near the creek. Being on the floor of an enclosed canyon, none of the animals were tethered. All she had to do was pick a relatively docile one, mount up and ride away. It was as simple as that . . . except that in life nothing ever is!

'You and me need to talk, colonel,' Jared Tucker rasped.

Ranald Mackenzie glanced sharply at the annoying individual who had abruptly appeared at his side. He had many concerns on his mind, but the most pressing was deciding when to turn his column towards its true destination. During daylight hours he had deliberately avoided Palo Duro Canyon. By apparently aimlessly roaming the surrounding barren terrain, he had hoped to persuade the Comanches that he didn't know of its existence. Now that the light was almost gone, he needed to send out the scouts to screen his movements. 'This is not a good time,' he retorted. 'I'll send for you if and when I can spare a moment.'

Tucker's eyes flashed dangerously. Here was a man not completely in control of his simmering rage. 'That just ain't good enough, mister. I ain't one of your enlisted men, bowing and scraping in front of you. You'll damn well have to make time!' As he spoke, his voice grew thoughtlessly loud.

Mackenzie immediately reined in, raw anger plain to see on his strained features. 'You forget yourself, Mister. . . ?'

'Tucker!' the other man angrily retorted.

The professional soldier nodded impatiently. 'Don't presume that your presence with this expedition gives you any special privileges. And keep your voice down in the presence of the enemy, or my sergeant major will club you senseless.' So saying, he gestured behind the civilian.

Startled, Tucker glanced round and saw the burly non-com sitting his horse, all the while covering him with a service revolver. Slightly chastened, but still determined, he did lower his voice as he tried again. 'I apologize, Colonel, but my daughter might be in the village that you're going to attack.'

Mackenzie's eyes narrowed slightly, but his expression remained just as hard and remote. 'There is that possibility.'

The civilian waited, but it seemed there was no more to come, and with that realization came renewed anger. 'Goddamnit! If your men go charging in, shooting at anything that moves, they could easily hit Lucy! Doesn't that bother you?'

The colonel sighed, although whether it was with regret or just irritation was not immediately apparent. 'Whatever you may think of me is irrelevant. I cannot and will not allow the needs of one civilian, however precious to you, to jeopardize this mission. The lives of too many settlers depend on my finally pacifying this land.' He paused, as though choosing his next words carefully. 'However, I am not an unreasonable man. I am also no stranger to death and suffering. If I had a daughter held captive in a Comanche village, I would no doubt feel as you do. So I will allow you to go in with the advance party. But, you will stay with Sergeant major Spikes here at all times. If he decides that you are a danger to the mission, he will knock you unconscious and put you in irons. Do you understand?'

Tucker again glanced at the poker-faced non-com and grimaced. 'Oh, I comprehend all right. And thank you, Colonel.'

Without another word, that man urged his mount forwards, his mind already on other matters. Spikes returned his revolver to its flap holster. 'Stay close, Tucker,' he brusquely ordered. 'Now it's dark, he'll be leading us over to the canyon. We'll be going in with Captain Beaumont's company. And remember what the colonel said. You step out of line, and I'll see that you end up bucked and gagged, so help me God!'

Tucker had served in the army. He well knew how unpleasant such a punishment was. 'That's a mite unfriendly. Why have you taken agin me, Sergeant Major?'

Keeping his voice low, that man responded, 'Because you were disrespectful to the colonel. He might well be an awkward, ornery son of a bitch, but he's my commanding officer, and a damn good one too. Just remember that, next time you feel like running off at the mouth, Mister Tucker!'

*

Lucy felt a surge of elation. She had made it to the vast pony herd without being discovered. Her only possession, other than the meagre skins that she wore, was a leather bridle, stolen on her way through the village. The animals were well used to human contact, and displayed no alarm as her slim form flitted amongst them. Although nervous at the prospect of having to ride bareback, she quickly identified a suitable mount. A piebald pony nuzzled her as she approached, and something about the apparently docile creature gave her confidence. This one would do.

Quickly slipping the bridle on, she whispered softly into its ear. Then, taking hold of a thick clump of mane, she swung up on to its back. The pony snorted mildly, but made no attempt to dislodge her. Safely astride her new mount, Lucy swiftly glanced back at the sleeping village. By the time they awoke, she would be long gone. She crushed a childish urge to laugh out loud. There would be time enough for that on the rim of the canyon.

A vicelike grip closed over her left ankle, sending a spasm of panic through her whole body. Before she could even react, the slip of a girl abruptly found herself flying sideways. Thrown clear of the piebald, her back hit the ground with stunning force. Winded and gasping, she had no opportunity to attempt a run for it. Peering down on her through the gloom in gleeful triumph was a teenage Comanche: one of the sturdy young pony herd guards she had completely missed.

Desperately sucking air into her lungs, Lucy

croaked, 'Please, please let me go. No one will know.'

The warrior-to-be understood all too well what she meant, even if not the actual words. Dropping into a crouch, he slapped her hard across the face, and then shook his head. As tears welled in her eyes, he again seized a slim ankle and began to drag his prisoner back to the village. Already anticipating the acclaim, he announced his achievement in ringing tones.

Within moments, curious villagers surrounded the two very different youngsters. Ominously, it was her chief tormentor who held sway. All the while patting the young buck in approval, the old crone rattled off a series of guttural sentences. If Lucy had thought that she might be merely chastised and returned to her ragged bed, she was about to be savagely disillusioned.

Moments later, the terrified girl found herself with her hands tied behind her back, and a rawhide thong being tightened around her throat. Hauled by the leash over to a wooden post sunk into the ground, the other end of the rawhide was tied to it, effectively immobilizing her. Then someone produced a quirt, and suddenly brutal entertainment took precedence over sleep.

Her meagre clothing was ripped off, and immediately the lash began to fall on to the tender flesh of her naked back. As the dreadful torment continued interminably, Lucy had no idea who was doing this to her, but even then it was obvious that she still hadn't completely given up hope, because intermingled with howls of pain, one word alone was audible. 'Papa!'

*

91

With the Tonkawa Scouts acting as a skirmish line to confuse the shadowing Comanches, the Fourth Cavalry had turned north and ridden without respite for five hours or so. Both men and animals were tired, but the humans knew better than to voice any complaints within earshot of their exacting commanding officer. Finally the column reached the rim of Palo Duro Canyon, unknown to any white men until Mackenzie's exploratory expedition two years earlier. As the huge, dark, gaping chasm stretched out before them, some of the men involuntarily crossed themselves at the prospect of having to descend to its floor and into the very jaws of death. Not only would the journey down be dangerous, but also they didn't know what they would encounter once they eventually got there.

Woodrow Clayton and Jared Tucker had moved up to join Captain Beaumont's company. Together at the edge of the cliff, yet apart from the soldiers, they stared down at the large Comanche village, hundreds of feet below. In the dim light, they could just about make out the individual hide lodges. There had to be a powerful number of people down there, although it was also possible that the warriors to defend it were amongst those whom they had already encountered. Which meant that they were somewhere out in the gloomy vastness behind them. Yet however the cavalry looked at it, one thing was for sure. Their colonel was definitely taking on an awful lot!

'Kind of makes you think, don't it?' Clayton quietly remarked.

Before his companion could respond, they were joined by the captain, who had some particular intelligence for the settler. 'I've spoken with one of the Tonks. Seems that the leader of the war party that hit your spread is called Buffalo Head. Kind of makes sense, with what you say he was wearing.'

Tucker stared at him intently. 'And is that his village, down there?'

The captain shrugged. 'Now that he didn't say. It's possible, but it's more likely to be Quanah Parker's. Thing is, there's only so much we know about what goes on out here, so don't get your dander up. This might sound harsh, and I'm sure I ain't the first to say it, but there's more at stake than just your daughter. If you should forget that, Spikes is under orders to remind you,' he added meaningfully.

Before Tucker could react, a rider arrived from Mackenzie. 'Colonel's compliments, sir. A goat trail has been discovered. You are to set off down it with your company immediately. Once on the canyon floor, you are to form a perimeter until the rest of the regiment joins you. On no account do you attack the village unsupported. Only if you are discovered are you to open the fight.'

Having said his piece and received an acknowledgement, the courier saluted and disappeared into the gloom. Beaumont glanced ominously at Tucker. 'Those orders were meant for me, but they apply to you as well.' Then he was gone, organizing his officers and men for the perilous task ahead.

*

93

As soon as Quanah Parker realized that the horse soldiers had turned north, he instinctively knew that they were making for Palo Duro Canyon. Which, of course, confirmed that 'Bad Hand' Mackenzie had to be in command, because it was that same tenacious bluecoat who had discovered the Comanche stronghold some twenty moons earlier.

Even as Quanah's heart lurched at the thought of his undefended family in the village on the canyon floor, the tactical opportunities also occurred to him. If he could position his warriors around the rim after the soldiers had descended, the white eyes might hopefully be caught like rats in a trap. As to the fate of their loved ones . . . well sometimes it was better not to think too much about a situation over which he had no control!

The steep descent down the precipitous path had been a living nightmare of heart-stopping missteps and gloom-shrouded crevices. The journey was made all the more difficult by the need to lead their horses down. Leaving them untended was out of the question, and faced with an unknown number of warriors, splitting the force to leave a rearguard on the rim also wasn't an option. As always, it was far harder negotiating unknown ground when moving down rather than up. Yet after sweating and cussing seemingly for a lifetime, the eighty-five men finally made it to the canyon floor. Somewhere behind them was the rest of the regiment, but they might as well have been on the moon for all the support they could provide in the event of immediate trouble.

From their new perspective, the enemy village was mostly concealed by the vast pony herd. As Captain Beaumont signalled for his men to spread out in a skirmish line, Jared Tucker edged to the front. The sweat coating his body had little to do with the harrowing scramble, and plenty to do with concern for the possible presence of his daughter. He was flanked by Clayton and Spikes, neither of whom was intending to let him out of their sight. Yet with the chance of their being discovered growing by the minute, Tucker couldn't stand it any longer.

Twisting round to face the sergeant major, he suddenly blurted out, 'If Lucy's in there, I've got to find her before your men open fire.'

Spikes swung his revolver over to cover the settler. 'I've got my orders, an' you ain't going anywhere, mister!'

Tucker had his Winchester ready to ward off any swinging blow. 'The only way you're gonna stop me leaving is by shooting me, and you really can't do that, can you?' Without waiting for a response, he abruptly turned away and moved off at speed in a half crouch. His heart was thumping at the prospect of a bullet in the back, but no shot rang out.

Sergeant major Spikes swore quietly but vividly before glancing angrily at Clayton. 'Me an' that pus weasel friend of yourn are gonna have a serious disagreement when this is all over.'

The other man sighed. 'As I keep trying to tell everyone, he isn't actually my friend.'

Perhaps it was the ever-present pain that dragged Lucy out of her drugged sleep. Or possibly it was the rawhide noose around her neck that made breathing increasingly difficult. Her dreadfully abused young body lay against the vertical post to which she was secured. Having tired of molesting her, the villagers had returned to their lodges and all was quiet. Shifting position slightly, she groaned out loud. Blood seeped from multiple cuts on her back, but whereas at one time she would have cried piteously, now she just felt numb.

The guards had returned to the pony herd, and darkness still coated the land. She was completely alone, but even in her misery she was able to realize and accept that she was unlikely to get another chance to escape. Now more than ever, she was totally reliant on her father fulfilling his shouted promise to her!

Given that, with a creek running off to his right, the only way to approach the village was through the pony herd, it was perhaps inevitable that Tucker would encounter one of the young guards who were habitually assigned to such a relatively menial task. As he slipped cautiously between the grazing animals, some of them detected a scent they were unfamiliar with and began to whinny. Anxiously speeding up, the intruder literally bumped into a slight figure coming towards him, and instinctively lashed out with his Winchester. The butt slammed into his victim's skull, knocking the Comanche down and out. Nervous ponies moved away, barging into each other in their haste.

In the still night air every sound carried, and from a few yards away a voice called out something incomprehensible. Tucker emitted a low grunt, but it obviously wasn't satisfactory because that individual came running, whilst at the same time calling out to someone else.

'Shit!' the settler muttered, and on a hunch dropped to the ground. He ran the risk of being trodden on, but the need to hold his fire overrode that. Whoever loosed off the first shot, he sure as hell didn't want it to be him.

The other sentry burst into the open space created by the disturbance, narrowly missing Tucker and instead tripped over his unconscious comrade. As the Indian lurched forward, his forefinger contracted around the trigger of his old smoothbore. Its sudden discharge seemed to split the night air, and as if that wasn't bad enough the massive lead ball struck one of the creatures that he was meant to guard. As the badly wounded pony noisily careered off into the night leaving a trail of blood, Tucker repeated the only word that seemed to do the situation justice: 'Shit!'

Just in front of him, the startled warrior was peering round for the cause of his mishap, yet still the white man didn't want to discharge his repeater. Swiftly drawing his knife, he launched himself across the gap that separated them. With tremendous force, he

landed on the much slighter figure, effectively immobilizing him. Without any hesitation, he repeatedly
rammed the blade into soft, yielding flesh. The
Comanche moaned once very loudly and then lay
twitching convulsively beneath him.

Tucker remained on top of the sparsely clothed
figure, in an almost sexual embrace, until all movement ceased. His nose twitched at the strong smell of
animal grease that came from his now lifeless prey,
and he was suddenly uncomfortably aware of the fresh
blood that coated his right hand. Only then did his
limbs begin to tremble slightly. It's a hell of a thing to
kill a man with cold steel, and despite his service in the
war this was an unwelcome first.

Fifty or so yards away, Sergeant Major Spikes was in no
doubt about what had just happened. 'The stupid
bastard's given us away,' he snarled.

As a professional hunter, firearms were something
that Clayton knew plenty about. 'That was no
Winchester. Sounded more like a muzzle-loader to me.'

In reality, it mattered little who was to blame. The
damage was irretrievably done.

Recognizing that any surprise had been lost,
Captain Beaumont bellowed out, 'Prepare to defend
yourselves,' and the well-trained troopers did just that.
The designated horse-holders dropped back with
their charges, whilst the remainder 'took a knee' and
levelled their carbines.

As the captain watched his men take up their posi-
tions in the gloom, a plan of action came to him. Since

his company's discovery was now inevitable, and he had no intention of advancing on the village unsupported, it made sense to start depriving the enemy of their most valuable resource.

'Open fire on the pony herd,' he ordered, before glancing hopefully back at the deserted goat trail. Surely the rest of the regiment would begin to join them soon. As his command was passed down the line, muzzle flashes lit up the night and the dreadful slaughter began.

Over in the village there was pandemonium, as the terrified inhabitants spilled out of their lodges, searching for the source of the gunshots. The first one had merely created mild concern, as it was not unknown for the young horse-herd guards to fire at shadows, but this was something else entirely. They had no idea who might be attacking them, because such an occurrence was inconceivable so far into the Llano Estacado. More specifically, a respected medicine man had assured the villagers that they would not be set upon.

With the absence of Quanah Parker and most of the warriors, their families would have been pretty much defenceless . . . except for the fact that earlier that day a war party led by Buffalo Head had arrived and been made welcome. He had come to join Quanah, hoping for a fight with the hated Texans. What he now had instead was a totally unexpected battle with the US Army. And since no Comanche would ever consider fighting on foot, his warriors raced to retrieve their ponies. They were nearest the lodges, and so relatively safe from Beaumont's fusillade. It was also a fact that they were the furthest point reached by a certain lone white man desperately searching for one of Buffalo Head's captives!

CHAPTER EIGHT

The sudden outburst of firing behind him took Jared Tucker by surprise. Just who the hell were the soldier boys shooting at? It was only as he scurried off to his right, towards the creek, to avoid any stray bullets that the army's newfound ruthlessness dawned on him. One couldn't gainsay the logic, though. On foot, the Comanches were apt to be a whole lot more reasonable.

The enforced detour probably saved his life in more ways than one, because as he dropped down the side of the creek bank, warriors began to spill out of the lodges. As they raced for their ponies, Tucker held his fire. He had a far greater priority than merely killing Indians. Then something happened that set his heart pumping fit to burst. A lone warrior stepped into the open, and even in the poor light there could be no mistaking the distinctive headdress that he pulled on. Buffalo Head! If this was his village, then Lucy had to be here!

In a half crouch, Tucker scrambled along the

banking, until he was level with the heart of the village. With the warriors abruptly absent, on their way to fight the army, it was just the chance that he needed. For sure, there were Comanches milling around the lodges, but they were women and old men. Now standing erect, he crested the bank and strode towards the settlement with his Winchester ready, for all the world to see as though he owned the place. He ached to bellow out his beloved daughter's name, but decided to get closer first. It would do neither of them any good for him to be shot by some trigger-happy squaw!

Although undoubtedly best qualified for the bloody task in hand, Woodrow Clayton had so far held his fire. Sharps cartridges didn't come cheap, and in any case he had a feeling that he would shortly have need of them for other prey. In truth, the troopers were shooting blind, thanks to the thick bank of powder smoke now covering their front. Then there came the fearsome pounding of unshod hoofs. Since the nearest members of the pony herd were either dead or scattered, this had to be something else, and Clayton for one prayed that Mackenzie and the main body would get down that track pronto.

'Cease firing!' Beaumont bellowed, since it behoved him to see what they were now up against.

Even as the smoke began to clear, a hellish chorus of howls and shrieks erupted, and suddenly every man in the company could see the horde of mounted savages charging directly at them.

'Jesus save us!' Spikes exclaimed, but in reality he would have to make do with the company commander, who thankfully happened to be more than capable.

'Volley fire on my command,' that individual shouted.

The Comanches timed their assault to perfection. Sweeping in at great speed, they seemed able to anticipate when the troopers would open fire. At just the right moment, they separated into two groups like water parting against a rock. The army carbines opened fire, but only those on either end of the line drew blood, and then not much.

Seemingly without even slowing their pace, the Indians then raced around the soldiers' flanks, with the intention of getting in close before they could reload their 'trapdoor' Springfields. The deadly plan had a good chance too . . . except for one thing. Many in Mackenzie's regiment, including Beaumont's company, had recently been issued with Spencer repeating carbines. Which was one reason why it was his men that made up the advance party. Although not as fast to operate as a Winchester, its seven-round magazine and rugged efficiency ensured that the horse Indians were about to get a nasty shook . . . so long as the troopers held their nerve.

A night attack by mounted, screaming berserkers was a terrible thing to withstand, but not a new experience for Mackenzie's men, who had been tempered by years under his relentless command. Stiffened by the officers and non-coms, the other ranks turned to face their flanks and unleashed a withering fire. Having only to work the under-lever and cock the hammer between shots, it meant that the Comanches received no respite. Savaged by heavy chunks of lead more than half an inch in width, they swiftly swung away, puzzled by the murderous rate of fire.

About to utter a great sigh of relief, Beaumont heard unexpected noises behind him and twisted about in horror. But the men approaching him wore blue wool jackets rather than breechclouts. He and his troopers were no longer alone in the enemy's stronghold, and for that he thanked God. He might well have held off though, had he been able to see beyond the rim!

As he approached the first of the widely spaced hide lodges, Jared Tucker suddenly had no thought for anything beyond the confines of the village. And yet, despite his obsession with finding Lucy, he had the wit to recognize that he had to be careful. Even old men and women were quite capable of pulling a trigger.

Everywhere was chaos. The continuous roar of gunfire had left the inhabitants in no doubt that they were in great danger. Since the nearest escape route was obviously compromised, there was little choice other than to grab children and belongings and flee deeper into the vast canyon. And then, from out of nowhere, a lone white man was abruptly in their midst.

'Lucy!' he cried out. 'Lucy, where are you, girl?'

A young woman with a child in her arms suddenly

appeared before him and her dark eyes met his. Twitching with surprise, she looked him up and down before unleashing a piercing scream.

Frustration began turning to anger. 'I'm not here to hurt you, God damn it,' Tucker protested. 'I'm just looking for a white girl, is all.'

The screaming continued, attracting unwanted attention from people already badly scared. And some of them were armed. An old man swathed in buffalo hide came from behind the shrieking female. In his gnarled hands was an ancient Hawken rifle, a fifty calibre that was still more than capable of bringing down anything on legs . . . and its hammer was fully cocked. Tucker didn't hesitate. His Winchester crashed out, and the elderly Comanche crumpled to the ground without a sound. Sadly, the gunshot, along with the woman's continued wailing, only served to increase the panic in the village. In the poor light, the terrified people couldn't discern how many assailants were upon them.

'Lucy!' he tried again, ever more loudly. 'It's your pa. I've come for you!'

As he blundered through the village, women and children fled from his approach until a shot rang out, and Tucker literally heard a projectile pass his head, sounding like a bee in flight. Dropping into a crouch, he peered around. Barely five yards away, a young boy was desperately struggling to cock a Colt Navy revolver. Although not the largest of Colt's many weapons, it appeared massive in his diminutive hands.

'Drop it!' the white man boomed. 'For Christ sakes

don't make me shoot you!'

The grimly determined child, perhaps thinking he was defending his mother, gritted his gleaming teeth and made a supreme effort. With an ominous double click, the hammer came back to full cock. Tucker emitted an anguished moan and fired. As the bullet shattered his young victim's skull in a welter of blood and brain matter, he turned away in disgust, sickened by what he had been forced to do. He had come to rescue his own child, not murder other people's!

Then the intruder heard the chillingly distinctive sound of pounding hooves, and he abruptly realized that it might soon be him that needed rescuing. Buffalo Head's warriors had obviously bitten off more than they could chew with Beaumont's troopers, and were returning to cover the evacuation of the village. And the sun was coming up, which was not necessarily a helpful thing in his situation. Furthermore, and unbeknown to them all, the beleaguered Comanches were about to receive some help.

Quanah Parker heard the gunfire and was puzzled. It sounded as if a full-on fight was taking place, rather than the sacking of a defenceless village. Could it be that another war party had providentially turned up out of the blue?

Moments later he was at the canyon's rim, and all became clear. Dawn's first rays were sufficiently strong for him to spot Buffalo Head's distinctive headdress. The bluecoats, who were now all down on the canyon floor, had stood off his warriors. Yet the soldiers presented perfect targets for the newcomers around the rim . . . if those Comanches were able to take full advantage.

With mixed feelings, Quanah ordered his followers to line the crest. Not all of them possessed modern weapons or even adequate ammuniton, but with any luck they had enough to make things very unpleasant for 'Bad Hand' and his men. It was a fact that the Indians were more adept at mobile warfare, but hopefully the soldier chief would rue the day that he had decided to lead his men deep into Comancheria!

Ranald Slidell Mackenzie peered about at the dispositions of his regiment. Such a man as he would never be entirely satisfied with anything, but there was no denying that his officers knew their business. As the men had arrived at the bottom of the precarious trail, one in four had taken control of the horses, whilst the remainder spread out behind Beaumont's troopers. Since their Spencers had easily seen off the only assault, it was obviously time to move on the village and do what they had come for.

The young colonel sighed and shifted uncomfortably in his saddle. Even a decade on, he was still grievously troubled by his various injuries. In particular was the shoulder wound received at the Second Battle of Manassas. He had been struck by a .52 calibre ball from a rifled musket that could quite easily have taken his arm off. As it was, the pain from it never left him. For a few moments he was unaccountably back amongst the booming cannon and blood-soaked terrain of the battleground in Virginia. For a young and impressionable officer it was like entering hell itself. And yet, the pulsating excitement was like nothing else he had ever experienced. Perhaps that was why he had remained in the army, because nothing else in life could ever match it.

Mackenzie blinked and shook his head. Sometimes, even in the midst of a battle, he just drifted off without realizing it. Possibly that was the price to be paid for surviving such horrors.

Warm liquid splashed on to his face, and he turned in surprise. His orderly, an elderly soldier named Pickens, who had served him for many years on the frontier, no longer possessed any recognizable features. A projectile from above had struck him in the back of his head. Flattening out, it had then exited bloodily through his lower jaw, narrowly missing Mackenzie as it did so. Even as he mopped the sticky fluid from his eyes, he instinctively glanced up at the rim. What he saw was disconcerting, but didn't really surprise him.

Others in the command took it less calmly. An enlisted man pointed up at the frightening array of Comanche warriors and wailed, 'Sweet Jesus, they'll kill us all!'

As if to confirm that statement, muzzle flashes showed along the edge and the whole command discovered that they were again under attack.

After calmly wiping the rest of the gore from his face, Mackenzie bellowed out for all to hear. 'There'll be no more talk like that, do you hear? I brought you all into this canyon, and I will take you all out again!'

Bizarrely, even the gunfire from the rim seemed to subside for a few moments after that. Then, as lead did again begin to kick up dirt around them, he snapped out a series of orders to his immediate subordinates. Roughly half the regiment under his overall command would advance on the village, whilst the rest would concentrate their fire on the assailants above them. There would be no withdrawal until they had achieved their objectives.

Woodrow Clayton turned to Spikes, a defiant look in his eyes. 'I'm going on to the village. I came here to help Jared get his daughter back, not just kill Indians.'

Surprisingly, the grizzled non-com nodded agreeably. 'Fair enough, mister. Those Comanche devils already know we're here, so there ain't much you two fellas can do to mess things up. But think on this. If he's all on his lonesome in the village, that girl might not even have a pa any more!'

As the mounted warriors thundered back to the village, Tucker looked around with increasing desperation. Alone and without the cloak of darkness, it would be suicide to remain where he was. Even though the non-combatants were now keeping clear of him, there had been no answer from Lucy to his loud cries. Yet that still didn't mean that she wasn't there. Tied up and gagged, she would have been incapable of responding. All he could do was stay alive and wait for the army to overrun the village.

Turning on his heels, he raced back to the creek

109

bank. It was too much to hope for that he wouldn't be spotted, yet the Comanches had more on their minds than just one lone white man. 'Bad Hand' was undoubtedly intent on destroying the village, and there were women and children to protect. So it was that only half a dozen warriors were sent to run him down.

With his chest heaving, Tucker dropped down on to the banking. Even though his pursuers were barely a pistol shot away, he deliberately held fire. Until he regained control of his breathing, he had little chance of hitting anyone, and every chance of wasting valuable cartridges. The one benefit in them getting nearer was that he was less likely to miss. In line abreast, the six Comanches swept towards him, misreading his silence for fear, and confident that his brutal death was a certainty.

Abruptly he popped up into view, and the death-dealing Winchester opened up at a staggering rate. At close range, and working the lever-action like a demon, Tucker cut down his assailants as though with a scythe. Three ponies collapsed in bloody distress, throwing their riders. The other three warriors instinctively veered away from a deadly situation that they hadn't anticipated. And yet it wasn't fear, by any means. More a superstitious reaction to the unexpected. The army's sudden acquisition of the Spencer was shocking enough, but the use of Winchesters against them was a rarity in Comancheria. And none of them yet realized that they had already done battle with this particular white man.

As those still mounted fled to the village, Tucker rapidly switched his attention to the survivors. One lay on the ground, either dead or stunned. The other two were well apart and already on their feet, sprinting towards him with their knives drawn. The realization that he couldn't get them both took only a split second to dawn on him, but it was still long enough to send a chill down his back. And yet fear didn't affect his logic. By aiming at the warrior on his left, it meant that he then had his rifle in a position to at least use it to block the other man's attack. Squeezing the trigger, he saw blood pump from his victim's chest as the man slewed sideways. He staggered on a few more steps, before dropping to his knees. If not a mortal wound, it had certainly stopped him in his tracks.

As he swung to his right, Tucker thrust the Winchester forward with both hands in the nick of time. There was a jarring crash, as the Comanche's knife blade collided with the forestock. The warrior was lean and leathery, with high cheekbones and murder in his dark eyes. Yet he was shaken and blown from the heavy fall, followed by a desperate run at his enemy. He had pinned everything on the knife thrust, and now just couldn't react in time. Tucker swung the Winchester's stock in a tremendous 'roundhouse' blow that caught the Comanche on the side of his skull. Abruptly helpless, that individual fell back, and Tucker followed it up by smashing the butt into his face, breaking his nose and effectively finishing the fight. He didn't even bother wasting a cartridge on him.

It was only then, now that he was no longer fighting for his life, that he perceived the outbreak of shooting on the rim, followed by answering fire from below. Then there came the welcome sound of a great many shod hoofs, as part of the Fourth Cavalry advanced on the village.

After glancing down at his vanquished opponent, Tucker left the creek bank and moved fast to join them. He hadn't yet given up on finding Lucy somewhere in the lodges, and didn't trust the soldiers' ability to distinguish between friend and foe. As he approached the third fallen warrior, who was apparently suffering with a badly fractured arm, that man frantically scrabbled for his firearm. Before desperately searching fingers could reach it, Tucker swung his rifle muzzle over to cover him. Without even breaking step, he fired a bullet into the Comanche's face, snuffing out his life in an instant. They were so close that powder burns also marked the warrior's shattered features.

Thereafter ignoring his latest victim, Jared Tucker single-mindedly maintained his rapid pace. He fully intended to be present when the cavalry hit the village. And yet, as it turned out, Woodrow Clayton had got there first. As Captain Beaumont's company reached the outlying lodges, they found the buffalo hunter cautiously moving from one to the other. Then, from off to his right, the startled officer saw the abducted girl's father stalking towards them.

'For pity's sake give me a chance to search for her!' Tucker demanded.

112

The captain impatiently reined in alongside his own screen of Tonkawa scouts, who were increasingly eager to pillage the enemy village. 'Just what makes you think she's here, Tucker?' he demanded. 'This isn't the only Comanche camp on the Staked Plains.'

'Because I've seen Buffalo Head,' the homesteader spat back. 'And it was his men that took her.'

Beaumont shook his head sadly, before glancing at one of the scouts. 'Tell him,' he ordered.

That particular Tonkawa stared at Tucker with obvious contempt. He had no love of white men, and was only accompanying the expedition because of the old adage: the enemy of my enemy is my friend. That and the chance for plunder, of course. Besides, someone who couldn't even look after his own children really wasn't worthy of considerations. 'This not Buffalo Head's village,' he barked. 'He come from other canyon further north.'

Tucker gazed at him in stunned disbelief. 'But how will he and his warriors get back to their own village?'

It was the scout's turn to register incredulity. 'Palo Duro plenty big. Many other trails out of here. They will know them all. You know nada!'

Despite his anger at the Indian's arrogance, Tucker felt himself floundering. Could all this death and struggle have been for nothing? It was simply too much to accept.

Then, in a flurry of activity, Colonel Mackenzie arrived to put the inevitable question. 'What is the delay, Captain Beaumont?'

That man glanced at the homesteader before replying. 'Mister Tucker wishes to single-handedly search the village before we move in. It has just been explained to him that if his daughter was seized by Buffalo Head's warriors, then she is unlikely to be here at all.'

The colonel glared down at the progressively more desperate parent. 'You test my patience, Mister Tucker. In case you hadn't noticed, there's a war taking place. So stand aside, or these men will ride you down with my blessing.' He then transferred his full attention to the captain, and his eyes gleamed with an almost frightening intensity as he issued his orders. 'I intend to finish what you started. Tell the Tonkawas they may take their pick of the remaining pony herd, and then you will kill everything else on four legs. And I mean everything! The only way to stop this cycle of violence once and for all is to put the Comanches afoot.'

Recognizing the horrified expression on his trusted subordinate's face, he added by way of explanation, 'Whenever we have captured Indian ponies in the past, they have always managed to retake them. Well, not this time. Not ever again! And burn the whole village. Lodges, blankets, robes, food. Anything that could sustain them through the winter.' With that, Mackenzie turned his mount and rode off to supervise the defence against Quanah Parker's warriors on the rim.

Simultaneously, the colonel's command was now engaging superior numbers that were also tactically better placed, as well as destroying everything of value to the enemy. Unfortunately, none of that took Jared Tucker any nearer to finding his child!

CHAPTER NINE

Even though he had many hundreds of warriors prepared to accept him as their pre-eminent war chief, Quanah Parker nevertheless seethed with frustrated anger. Great plumes of smoke rose from the extended village that was his home, as the Comanches accumulated belongings were put to the torch. Ironically, much of it had been supplied by the US Government, through the Indian Agent at Fort Sill, as a way of 'buying' a fragile peace for the afflicted frontier.

Far worse than the burning of their lodges, though, was the bloody destruction of the pony herd. Never before had anyone slaughtered their animals on such a scale. Not even the Spanish, and their ruthlessness in warfare had been legendary. And because of the blue-coats' accurate repeating carbine fire, it was becoming clear that there was little Quanah could do about it. One of his problems was that although some of his warriors did in fact own Henry and Winchester repeaters, they possessed very few cartridges for them. Being unable to make their own, they were mostly dependent upon renegade white traders and Comancheros, and the army had been coming down hard on such people. He recognized that his best chance to gain retribution was to attack the soldiers as they returned up the precipitous trail, because it was unlikely that they would discover any of the canyon's other access points. But of course by then, their deadly work would be done.

Down in the canyon, volley after volley crashed out, but even that couldn't completely drown out the pitiful cries of wounded animals. Many of the troopers were being used to round up the terrified animals and force them towards the guns of their comrades, so that none would escape. The dismal sounds continued relentlessly, and they were like a knife in Quanah's guts. He recognized only too well that Bad Hand's actions that day could well result in him having to lead his people on to the despised government reservation, to tend small plots of land and eat watered-down beef rations issued by the profiteering Indian agent. No longer would they be able to carry out marvellous, extended raids throughout Texas and Mexico, or hunt the buffalo. Then again, those great beasts were fast disappearing off the plains, victim to the hated hide hunters that he had tried so hard to kill at Adobe Walls. All of this Quanah Parker could see, and it made his heart bad.

With smoke clouds rising all around them, and almost continuous gunfire in the background, the two civilians desperately worked their way through the chaotic

117

village. It was a hellish situation to be sure, but it could have been far worse. Although the troopers were slaughtering all the livestock, there was no equivalent butchery of people. Unlike the Sand Creek massacre ten years earlier in Colorado, where undisciplined volunteers had killed and mutilated scores of women and children, the non-combatants were allowed to drift away deeper into the canyon. Mackenzie was no murderer, and he knew full well that with the coming of winter his actions had been enough to drive the Comanches on to the reservation, which was all that had been asked of him.

Eventually it became apparent, even to Jared Tucker, that Lucy was not in the village. And after the Tonkawa's disclosure about Buffalo Head, it also seemed unlikely that she would be with the fugitives fleeing from it. Frustration was beginning to turn into despair!

Shouting to make himself heard over the continuous fusillade, Tucker impatiently questioned Captain Beaumont. 'What will happen after you have finished here?'

The captain, who had many calls on his time, nevertheless did his best to remain civil. 'We will fight our way out of here.'

'And then?'

'That will be up to the colonel.'

'Will he pursue Buffalo Head?'

Beaumont shrugged. 'That's not for me to speculate.'

'God damn it all to hell!' Tucker exploded. Spittle

flew from his lips and there was a wild look to his eyes. 'So where does that leave me, apart from between a rock and a hard place?'

The officer sighed regretfully. He was not unsympathetic to the other man's awful predicament, but he was in no position to offer assistance. 'In my opinion, Buffalo Head and his warriors will return to his village and move it immediately, because he will expect us to pursue him. Which means, if you are to go after them with any chance of success, you will need to leave immediately and catch them before the entire band disappears deeper into the Llano Estacado. That is what I think!'

Tucker glanced at Clayton. That individual had not said anything for a long time. 'Then it's obvious. I must leave now.'

'You mean we,' Clayton retorted. 'I ain't given up on you yet. But as I see it, there's one big problem. Neither of us know where that horned bastard has his village.'

A guttural voice immediately behind them caught them both unawares. 'I know!'

The civilians twisted around to find a Tonkawa scout regarding them through fathomless eyes. 'I know,' he repeated.

'But will you show us?' Tucker queried dubiously. He had little faith in Indians of any tribe, but he also had little choice. As hope of finding Lucy seemed to be receding, he was prepared to try anything.

The Tonkawa, who was armed with a battered 'Trapdoor' Springfield, motioned towards Tucker's distinctive Model 1866 Winchester. 'For that. And many cartridges.'

Tucker's eyes widened in surprise. He pondered for a moment, but really there was nothing to think about. 'Once I have her back. Then you can have it. You have my word. And cartridges.'

The Indian grunted, as though not placing any great value on a white man's word, but eventually nodded his agreement.

Tucker turned to Beaumont. 'Will you release him to me?'

Despite the fraught situation, the captain chuckled. 'Nothing I could say would make him do anything he didn't want to. The Tonks might officially work for the army, but they come and go as they please. They always have. So take him and be lucky.' He nodded briefly at the former scout, before making one last comment. 'Now for Christ's sake leave me be to do my job!'

Buffalo Head led his warriors up through the narrow defile at a breakneck pace that only expert riders born to the life could maintain. His only thought was to get back to their village in Tule Canyon, and then move it before the horse soldiers found it . . . as they inevitably would. The cursed Tonkawas would surely see to that! The only problem with having subjugated all the other tribes around Comancheria, was that some of them took every opportunity to get revenge by working for the increasingly ascendant 'white eyes'.

Even as he deftly controlled his pony, the war chief

pondered on where to take his people. With even the desolate 'Staked Plains' apparently no longer safe, he unknowingly began to emulate Quanah Parker by considering the unthinkable. The prospect of life on a white man's reservation had always been abhorrent to him. Being answerable to a corrupt Indian agent whilst farming small plots of poor land held no appeal, but at least the little ones wouldn't starve to death in the winter. And he too knew that the buffalo that had always provided for their every need were becoming less numerous, and he also knew the reason why.

Finally bursting out of Palo Duro Canyon, well clear of both the soldiers and Quanah's warriors, Buffalo Head no longer had any desire to join forces with his fellow leader. He had lost too many followers in the canyon and now thought only of their long-term survival. And it was as he and his men rode north to their threatened home that an idea came to him.

The young white girl that they had captured on their recent murder raid! If they took her with them to the agent in Fort Sill, they might just be able to extract more favourable terms. Suddenly, he fervently hoped that the old women hadn't too severely mistreated her, or marked her too visibly. Then, with a start, he recalled breaking her nose and he blanched slightly. It was a sad fact that the Americanos grew strangely angry when white captives of the Comanches were returned in poor condition, when really they should just be grateful to have them back. He would definitely have to give the matter more thought!

The three riders, one Indian and two white men, emerged from Palo Duro Canyon about one hour after the fugitive Comanches ... except, of course, they couldn't know that.

'You sure it's them?' Tucker shouted across to the Tonkawa.

That man nodded. 'Only riders to leave canyon ahead of us,' he yelled back in broken English.

'How far ahead?'

That was greeted by a silent shrug.

'I thought you was supposed to be a scout,' Tucker retorted sourly, but his comment was lost in the noise of pounding hooves. They were pushing the animals harder than was sensible, but he was driven by the knowledge that they only had a very small window of opportunity.

Behind them, the sounds of gunfire gradually receded in the distance, but showed no signs of slackening off. Woodrow Clayton glanced at Tucker's intense features and did just wonder if they were soon to bite off more than they could chew. If no soldiers from Mackenzie's command followed on, it would mean that the three of them would be up against an entire village of hostiles, and unfortunately his tortured companion appeared to be up for it. The hide hunter shook his head at his own foolhardiness. He was genuinely beginning to wish that he'd listened to James Hanrahan and remained at Adobe Walls with his compatriots, but it wasn't his way to just cut and run. He damn well hoped that this Lucy was still alive, though. Otherwise they were heading into a world of hurt for nothing!

Accompanied by a cloying acrid stench, the great sulphurous cloud of powder smoke hung over the canyon floor and mercifully obscured, if only temporarily, the grotesque mass of blood-soaked animals. Nothing like it had ever been seen on the plains before. Even the buffalo killed by professional hunters were at least spaced out over the landscape. Once decomposed, the slaughtered ponies would be fit only for use as a source of fertilizer . . . but that was to be some time in the future.

The village itself had been completely destroyed, and was also covered by a pall of smoke. Hide lodges, buffalo robes and army blankets supplied by the Indian Department had all fed the flames. Those with a discerning nose might even have detected the scent of burning buffalo meat, along with scorched flour and sugar.

The overall dismal mess seemed to have affected the Comanches up on the rim, because their gunfire had noticeably slackened off. Or perhaps they were just running short of cartridges. Either way, they appeared incapable of halting the army's relentless activities. And so, with nothing left to accomplish in the canyon, Mackenzie now had only to get his regiment, along with its wounded and their few prisoners, back up the steep path and clear of Palo Duro. Whether they would still be under threat after that was anybody's guess.

Even in daylight, with the trail no longer a mystery, it took more than an hour for the entire column to return to the rim, and all of that time they had been under desultory fire from Quanah's warriors. Yet strangely, given the vulnerability of the troopers' situation, the Comanches made no attempt to launch an all-out attack as they clambered up to the crest. It was as though Mackenzie's single-minded and unwavering action had somehow sapped the Indians of the will to resist. And yet one particular individual had it in mind to demonstrate that their spirit was not completely broken. One quite outstanding warrior chief!

As the weary, sweating soldiers finally reached level ground, their formation was not unnaturally disorganized. One unfortunate trooper in the vanguard, a Private Seander Gregg, was having difficulty in keeping up with his horse. The creature had badly bruised a foot during the arduous assent, and desired only to stop in an attempt to ease its pain. Instinctively spotting his enemy's vulnerability, Quanah Parker immediately leapt on to his pony and raced towards the struggling Gregg. That man was at first completely oblivious to the deadly threat approaching at speed. Only when the man behind him shouted a warning did he glance over towards the Comanches. What he saw left him horror struck and trembling.

An unusually large and well-muscled Indian was galloping directly for him brandishing a six-shooter. His bronzed body was daubed with ochre, and even at a distance he presented a vision of raw power and menace. Other soldiers saw the danger and opened fire, but they were still too few and too disorganized. In response to the gunshots, Quanah began to zigzag his pony, but all the time he remained focused on his particular target.

Gregg fumbled desperately with his carbine, but controlling his mount made taking any kind of aim nigh on impossible. And the animal's erratic movements meant that they were actually hampering the men behind him. As Quanah pounded across the flat land, he cocked his stolen Colt Army and revelled in the exhilaration of the moment. All he needed was one good kill shot.

'Shoot him, for Christ sake!' bellowed one of the troopers behind Gregg.

The terrified enlisted man finally succeeded in retracting the hammer, but then found himself facing the wrong direction, as his horse pawed at the ground with his injured leg. By that time, his frightening assailant was closing rapidly, to the extent that Quanah Parker's very proximity to Gregg protected him from the other troopers. The soldier's only realistic hope of survival was to throw himself from the horse, but the devil that was indecision held him in its grip.

Quanah levelled his revolver, and with the distance down to barely five yards, squeezed the trigger. There was a satisfying crash, and the bullet slammed into the bridge of Private Gregg's nose. Even as the piece of soft lead flattened out and made its exit from the back of his head in a geyser of blood and brain matter, Quanah expertly swung his mount away and urged it back towards his waiting comrades. Despite the very real danger of a bullet in the back, his heart was thumping from excitement rather than fear. Warfare truly could be a glorious experience!

From his delighted warriors, a great whoop of joy erupted. Amazing displays of bravery by their leader were far from unusual, but this latest exploit had been truly inspiring. By the time Seander Gregg's twitching body had toppled from his troubled horse, the war chief was already zigzagging to safety.

None of this dazzling bravado could alter the overall outcome, however. With Mackenzie's regiment safely out of the canyon, the Comanches could only attempt 'hit and run' raids against them. And the onset of winter would inevitably see the Indians and their families in dire straits. It had been an excellent result for the dour young colonel, but depending on his viewpoint there might still be one piece of unfinished business, the subject of which was about to be broached by one of his most trusted subordinates.

Eugene Beaumont guardedly viewed his commanding officer. 'Do you intend to pursue Buffalo Head, sir?'

The colonel's eyes narrowed slightly, which was about as much emotion as one might reasonably expect him to display. He was well used to concealing his almost continuous discomfort from others. 'To what purpose, captain? This has been hot work, but I am convinced that the savages are broken. The arrival of winter will see them all on the reservation, you mark my words.'

The captain sighed. 'That man Tucker is still searching for his daughter, sir. He and his friend have gone after Buffalo Head.'

Mackenzie's deadpan expression never altered. 'By "friend", I presume you mean the Tonkawa scout that you prematurely released from service.'

Despite the situation, Beaumont struggled to suppress a smile. Even with hundreds of men under his command, and constant demands on his time, the colonel didn't miss a thing. 'No sir. I mean the hide hunter, Clayton.'

'Ah, him,' Mackenzie muttered, as though suddenly considering him for the first time. 'Now that man has definitely been of service to the Fourth. The question is, does that fact warrant sending a force deeper into the Llano Estacado to assist them?'

CHAPTER TEN

Lucy Tucker had been tethered like a dog by a leash around her slim neck for over twenty-four miserable hours, and was no longer even aware of her surroundings. She had been given water to keep her alive, but that had been the limit of her spiteful captor's generosity. As a consequence, the pathetic child, unable to shift position more than a few inches in any direction, had even to endure the sight and smell of her own urine and excrement. Weak and disorientated, Lucy no longer had the strength to cry out. And yet somewhere in the recesses of her mind she still held on to the belief that her father would come for her. So when she first heard the sound of thundering hooves, it dimly occurred to her that she was being rescued, and her eyelids flickered open.

The frightening sight of Buffalo Head leading his warriors back into the village swiftly disabused her of that cherished hope. And yet, quite unbelievably, she wasn't that far off the mark. The instant that he saw Lucy's condition, the leader's anger erupted . . . and mercifully it was not directed at her. Almost incandescent with rage, he bellowed at the old woman who had made her life such misery. The hag stared up at the imposing war chief with a mixture of disbelief and real fear, but she wasn't given any time to ponder his baffling change in attitude. Buffalo Head rattled off a series of commands that created a hive of activity around him, and immediately brought about a massive improvement in the girl's circumstances.

The restraint was removed from around Lucy's neck at the same time as the bonds around her wrists were cut away, and then she was gently picked up by her particular warrior and carried over to a soft bed of furs. Here she was given delicious and highly nutritious pemmican, as well as a chunk of buffalo tongue, which was considered to be a great delicacy by both Indians and whites. As her circulation returned, the pain in her wrists was awful, but somehow she held back any tears. It was almost as though she was getting used to absorbing pain. Besides which, despite her weakened state, her attention was taken by the frantic hustle and bustle.

The whole village was being dismantled with great speed. Lodge poles were stacked and the hide coverings rolled up. Travois were attached to some of the many surplus ponies in the great herd and loaded with the tribe's belongings. Even for someone ignorant of Comanche language and behaviour, it was obvious that something traumatic had occurred, and that the entire settlement was preparing to flee.

When finally the village no longer existed and it

came time to move Lucy, surprising consideration was again shown to her. Since it was obvious to all that she couldn't yet ride, rather than tying her over the back of a pony as before, the girl's original captor laid her carefully on a travois and covered her with a US Government issue blanket. The reasoning behind this sudden display of kindness was just too obscure, because on the other occasions that he had touched her, there had been a great deal of self-gratification involved. Nevertheless, for the moment at least, she was content to just lie there and wait on events.

Barely was she settled, when Buffalo Head yelled a command and the whole tribe set off along the canyon floor in an extended column. Lying at an angle, with the ends of the two poles dragging on the ground, Lucy felt all the bumps and undulations, but this mode of travel was still far more comfortable than being strapped over an animal with her mouth full of its hair. As they progressed, she occasionally got a glimpse of the old squaw scowling at her, but it did seem that, for the present at least, she was out of her clutches.

Those warriors in the lead had already started climbing the steep trail that led out of the canyon. Others of their ilk were controlling the pony herd, but of course the pace of the evacuation was governed by that of its slowest members, and so Buffalo Head had to temper his natural impatience. He was consoled by the thought that even 'Bad Hand' would not have been able to extricate his troopers from Palo Duro and then follow on in the time available. And once out of this canyon, the Comanches would soon be able to disappear into the trackless wastes, and woe betide any cursed Tonkawas that might attempt to track them!

As a great void opened up before them, all three men gratefully dismounted. For many hours they had maintained a steady pace across the featureless, unyielding terrain, and the animals were about done in. To give him his due, the former army scout had led them unerringly to the right place, but that didn't mean their trust in him was complete. Far from it in fact.

Woodrow Clayton gestured for his companion to hang back slightly, so as to let the Tonkawa move beyond casual earshot. 'Whatever happens here, don't let that savage get behind you. He might be working for us right now, but I've heard dark things about his kind.'

Jared Tucker sighed impatiently. It was obvious he hadn't really got time for anything that didn't relate to rescuing Lucy. 'What things?' he managed.

'Only that they've been known to cook and eat their victims. Apparently, the Comanches nearly wiped them out, so they will do anything to get back at them . . . but they don't take to our kind a whole lot better.'

'Oh great!' the homesteader exclaimed. 'So I've promised my Winchester to a cannibal, have I?'

Clayton grunted. 'Just watch your back, is all.' With that, he ground-tethered his horse, and then moved up to join the Indian. Notwithstanding his previous comments, he decided that there was something he should know. 'If we are to fight together, it is only right that we know your given name,' he quietly remarked.

The Tonkawa's unreadable eyes settled on his for a moment, before he nodded. 'I am known as Choyopan. And do not be too quick to pick a fight, white man. They are many and we are few.' So saying, he stepped aside and motioned towards the canyon floor.

Hundreds of feet below, in an eerie reproduction of Palo Duro, were many scores of Comanches. But there was one big difference from Mackenzie's discovery: the village itself no longer existed. Its occupants, along with all their possessions, were on the move. In fact the vanguard was already ascending the narrow trail. Whatever the three men were intending, they didn't have much time.

Tucker joined them on the rim. He had heard the Tonkawa's last comment, but chose to ignore it. Instinctively he covered the shiny brasswork on his 'Yellow Boy' Winchester, so that the bright afternoon sun would not reflect on it. As he stared down at the Comanche horde, his eyes gleamed with the sadly all too familiar feverish intensity.

'She's down there. I can feel it,' he muttered fixedly.

Clayton was having none of that. 'That's what you reckoned at the other village. Maybe you just feel it because you want to,' he remarked.

Tucker's gaze never shifted, but his heated response was immediate. 'What the hell do you mean by that?'

The other man had no intention of being browbeaten. 'Don't go getting your dander up with me.

What I mean is, there's no way you can actually see her down there. Which means it's wishful thinking. And I can understand that, but is it enough for us to tangle with so many of them?'

'That's what we came here for, ain't it?' Tucker retorted, before gesturing towards Choyopan. 'And don't be fooled by what he said, because it's certainly what he came for. He hates them, remember?'

Clayton exhaled noisily. 'OK, OK.'

'Enough talk,' the Tonkawa hissed. 'We stop them before they get up here, or not at all!'

There was no gainsaying that, and so the three men moved over to a jumble of rocks near where the trail crested the rim. It was the only broken ground for miles around, and a true godsend. There was enough cover for them to stay hidden, and yet still inflict a great deal of damage on the exposed Comanches.

'Are there any other ways out of this canyon?' Tucker demanded of the Tonkawa.

Choyopan grunted. 'Nearest is half a day's ride, more for you.'

'That's it then,' the white man retorted, choosing to ignore the veiled insult. 'If they believe that Mackenzie is coming to attack them, then they'll want to stick with this path. We can offer a trade. Lucy in exchange for clear passage.'

'And if they won't deal?' Clayton demanded.

'What is it with you?' Tucker challenged. 'Nobody said this was gonna be easy. Maybe you should have stuck with shooting buffalo.'

'And maybe you should shut your God-damn

133

mouth,' the hunter angrily rejoined. 'I just don't relish seeing my scalp hanging from some lodge pole, is all!'

Choyopan stared at the two white men in disbelief. At a time like this, all they could do was squabble. Yet they thought of him as a savage! 'No time for such,' he growled. 'Comanches to kill.' And crouching down he moved off into the rocks.

'He's right,' muttered Tucker, somewhat shame-facedly. 'To have any chance of a parley, we need to stop them on that path. Are you still with me?'

'What kind of question's that? Of course I bloody am,' Clayton snapped, and so together they followed the Tonkawa into cover.

The three of them squatted down and quietly checked over their weapons. The time for talking had temporarily passed. They needed to be able to negoti-ate from a position of strength, which meant that there would have to be some killing. The nearest Comanches were approximately two hundred yards away and moving slowly up the steep incline. Such a shot would be child's play for the buffalo hunter.

'I figure we need to hit them hard,' Tucker opined. 'Leave the front-runners to Choyopan and me. Take down one further back. That'll maybe give them pause about who they're up against. Yeah?'

Clayton squinted against the sunlight and nodded. 'I reckon so.'

Choyopan merely grunted and retracted the hammer on his Springfield. Although only single shot, it could still pack quite a punch in the right hands.

The entire tribe of hostiles was now spread out on the exposed path out of Tule Canyon, and try as he might, Tucker still hadn't spotted his daughter. There were plenty of mounted youngsters visible, but none with her light colouring. Because it never occurred to him to scrutinize the primitive conveyances, his anxious gaze didn't linger on the vast numbers of travois being dragged behind ponies to transport the belongings. It might have surprised him to know that before they had acquired such creatures from the Spanish, the Comanches had used dogs for such a task.

As the Indians drew inexorably closer, Clayton adjusted the ladder sight on his Sharps and drew a fine bead on a warrior about ten places back from the front. With the butt tucked tightly into his shoulder, he breathed slowly and steadily, and then suddenly held it. Having already contracted the first of the double set triggers, the second required only the slightest squeeze.

As the loud gunshot rang out on the rim of the canyon, Clayton's victim fell sideways from his mount and tumbled headlong down the precipitous slope. The Comanches were given no time to react before two more shots crashed out. The bullet from Choyopan's Springfield struck the lead warrior in his stomach, causing him to double over yet remain mounted. After his first shot, which also claimed a fatality, Tucker wasn't too concerned with accuracy. His intention was to create the impression of greater numbers, and so he scrambled from rock to rock, firing off a round from each spot. Only after emptying the whole cylindrical magazine did he necessarily cease firing.

With the rocks now blanketed in powder smoke, Choyopan had only one comment to make. 'White man use too many cartridges. Less for me!'

Tucker snorted. 'This piece ain't yourn yet!'

Answering fire came from the Comanches, but taken by surprise their response was wild and ineffective.

'I reckon we've given them to know our intentions is serious,' Clayton yelled out as he reloaded his 'buffalo gun'. 'Question is, how are they gonna take it?'

The sudden volley of shots came as a grievous shock to Buffalo Head, and yet he was still level-headed enough to realize that there was no way 'Bad Hand' could have got his 'horse soldiers' to Tule Canyon so quickly. So this had to be something else entirely.

White men under attack in such a situation would most likely have dismounted and sought whatever cover there was available, to then respond with relatively disciplined carbine fire. The same was not true of Comanches. They instinctively remained mounted at all times, and this was to be no different. Unable to retreat because the trail was blocked with families, travois and the pony herd, by their reckoning they were left with no option other than to attack. Which was what they did . . . immediately.

*

'Holy shit!' Clayton exclaimed, as he watched the warriors frantically urge their ponies up the narrow track. 'They must be plumb loco.'

Tucker was still cramming fresh cartridges through the loading gate of his Winchester, but for the moment that didn't matter. With the Comanches unable to get more than two abreast at any point on the trail, his companions' breechloaders were initially quite sufficient to disrupt the charge. Choyopan fired first, wisely choosing an animal as his target, to cause maximum disruption. His aim was true, and with blood pumping from its chest, the stricken pony collapsed across the entire width of the path. Her rider took a crushing fall down the vertiginous canyon wall that was impossible to recover from. His broken body kept on twisting and rolling until finally it settled, a bloody and mangled mess, on the canyon floor.

Woodrow Clayton, well used to cherry-picking his targets, demonstrated his ability by placing a bullet right between the eyes of another warrior at the front. That man also ended up like a pulverised rag doll although, having died instantly, he hadn't suffered during the brutal descent.

Then Tucker again opened up with rapid fire, and the short-lived assault came to a swift and predictable end. With the way forward blocked, the Comanches had to resort to wasting valuable cartridges in an attempt to keep their attacker's heads down. As clouds of acrid smoke began to obscure the trail, Tucker decided that it was high time to open negotiations.

'Are you able to speak with them?' he demanded of

the Tonkawa.

That was greeted by an affirmative nod.

'Tell them that we are many, and that I have come for the captive white girl named Lucy. Tell them she is all I want from them. If they hand her over, there will be no more shooting and we will simply leave. Tell them.'

Even as Choyopan absorbed all that, Clayton muttered only half to himself, 'An' what if we're shit out of luck, an' she ain't even down there?'

If the desperate parent had heard that, he showed no sign. All his attention was on the Tonkawa, as that individual remained out of sight but bellowed some form of salutation down the trail. A few more shots rang out before finally relative silence settled. Only then did he show himself. Choyopan must have been pretty confident of both the Comanches curiosity and poor marksmanship, because he stood up in full view. Then, with a bizarre mixture of signs and languages, apparently launched into an explanation for his presence on the rim.

The concealed white men were able to make out certain words. Mucho hombre and nino were amongst the few discernible snippets. After saying his piece, the guide fell silent and waited. A reply was not long in coming. From some distance down the trail came a strong, authoritative voice.

Choyopan turned to Tucker. 'Stand up. Buffalo Head demands to see the man who hunts him.'

The homesteader didn't much relish coming under the Comanches' guns, but there was little choice if they were to make any progress. Rising up to his full height, he stepped out into the open and gazed over at his hated foe. With his distinctive headdress, the chief was easy to locate. That man stared back at him with shocked recognition, before barking out a series of guttural sentences at the Tonkawa.

'So what's the bastard got to say for himself?' Tucker demanded.

Still keeping his eyes on the Comanches, Choyopan half turned, but before he could speak, something truly momentous occurred.

The intake of nourishing food, along with an inherently strong constitution, meant that Lucy was no longer as weak as her captives thought. The gunshots had jerked her awake, and had her peering up at the rim, along with all the Comanches. The appearance up there of yet another savage meant nothing to her, but then quite amazingly her father came into view. For a brief moment she couldn't quite believe her eyes. Could it really be him? It was just too wonderful to comprehend.

'Pa!' she yelled out. 'Pa, you've come for me!'

Buffalo Head glared at her angrily, but when one of his warriors moved to strike her, he sharply rebuked him. Circumstances had dramatically changed. This white girl was no longer just a slave to be used up or traded away to the Mexicans south of the border. She was now very definitely a valuable bargaining tool, and he needed time to think.

Up on the rim, Jared Tucker was ecstatic with

relief. 'My God!' he exclaimed. 'It's really you!' And yet even at a distance, Lucy seemed somehow different. Her face appeared strangely distorted. 'Are you . . . all right, my baby?' All right seemed such an inadequate question. 'Have they harmed you in any way?'

For whatever reason, there was no immediate answer to that, and the silence was ominous in itself. Yet he was given no chance to question her further, because Buffalo Head had much more to say to the hated Tonkawa.

After listening intently, Choyopan again glanced at his 'employer'. 'He says he remembers you. You shoot good with that long gun. My long gun. You can have the girl back . . . but only when all his people are out of the canyon. Oh . . . and he doesn't believe that we are many!'

Tucker chose to concentrate on the single relevant sentence in Choyopan's translation, and shook his head emphatically. 'No deal. We've only got the edge while they're bottled up on that path. You know I'm right. Those devils get up here, an' we're all as dead as one of Woody's buffalo.' Turning to that man, he added, 'What do you reckon?'

Clayton grinned ruefully. 'I got a plan of sorts, but it's mighty risky. Then again. . . .' He left that unfinished, because everything that had happened in the last few days had been mighty risky. 'Anyhu, what I thought was. . . .'

Having heard him out, Tucker also recognized the severe danger . . . for Lucy. But he didn't see that they had any choice. Fixing his full attention on the Tonkawa, he remarked, 'Tell that son of a bitch that I must talk with my daughter first before I decide. I must know that she is not injured.'

Choyopan regarded him sceptically. Not having fully understood all of Clayton's rapid speech, he could not see what difference her condition made to anything, but nevertheless did as instructed. The response when it came did not require translation. Buffalo Head merely nodded imperiously.

Tucker moved closer to the edge. He could see Lucy on her travois, and feared for the worst. 'Why are you on that contraption, girl? What have they done to you?'

There was an awful silence for a few seconds before she answered. Her voice trembled with emotion, and it seemed that she might burst into tears. 'They hurt me, pa. They hurt me real bad. So many times.' Then her tone grew stronger, as she added, 'But I'll be OK. You just see if I ain't.'

Jared Tucker could feel his chest tightening, as raw anger surged through his body. It took a supreme effort of will to appear outwardly calm, but he had no choice. What he said next would be critical, because he had no way of knowing how much American the Comanches could understand.

'I know you will, Lucy. But first we have to get you home.' He paused, before adding in a deceptively lighter tone, 'Do you remember the game we used to play when you were little? The one that was you and Samuel's favourite?'

For a moment Lucy stared up at him uncompre-hendingly. Then it dawned on her. Hide and seek! Her pa wanted her to make a run for it, away from these terrible folks. But where to go?

CHAPTER ELEVEN

Buffalo Head, impatient and uncomprehending, had heard enough. Growing increasingly fearful over the likely arrival of 'Bad Hand' and his troopers, he desperately needed to get his people out of the canyon. Bellowing up to the Tonkawa cur, he demanded an end to this foolishness. If they were not given immediate passage, the girl would die ... painfully and unpleasantly!

Although still very young, over the past few days Lucy had matured well beyond her years. Even though unable to understand his words, she could see the anger on Buffalo Head's brutalized features, and recognized that if she was to make a move, then it had to be straightaway.

'When she gets off the path, can you and that Sharps protect her?' Tucker asked, with a touch of desperation in his voice.

Clayton, still concealed from the Comanches, patted his precision weapon. 'Don't you worry none about that.' So saying, he retracted its hammer and waited for something to happen.

The old woman, still embittered over the killing of a relative by the white eyes, somehow sensed that the girl was about to make a move. With a malicious gleam in her eyes, she surreptitiously edged over towards the travois, a skinning knife in her right hand. Yet when the moment came, the hag was ill prepared to handle a youngster hell bent on gaining her freedom.

Lucy threw the fur blanket aside, and catapulted herself off the primitive conveyance. Knowing that her only chance lay in getting off the trail, she dashed for the edge . . . and crashed full on into the old woman. The girl's youthful momentum was sufficient to knock her vicious tormentor off her feet and down the steep, rocky slope. There was one brief scream, before the Comanche's scrawny body struck a rock headfirst. The solid object brought her fall to an abrupt end . . . along with her life.

Even as Lucy scrambled down the stony incline, her father was hollering advice. 'Use the body as cover and stay low!'

All the time struggling to keep her balance, the terrified girl made her way down to the fresh corpse. From behind her there came a deal of shouting, but she didn't dare turn to look.

Woodrow Clayton watched intently as Tucker's daughter fled, only she wasn't the main focus of his attention. The chief appeared to bark out a command, because one of his warriors rapidly dismounted and lunged after her. Even as he took swift aim, the professional hunter was accounting for his victim's size and speed. The lithe Comanche was already tackling the tricky descent when the Sharps crashed out. The heavy bullet tore into his right hip, shattering the ball and socket joint, and causing him to collapse in agony.

Lucy was initially unaware of the frantic activity behind her. So steep was the slope that it took all her concentration just to remain upright. Then she reached the old woman's bloodied cadaver, and dropped down to the rear of it. Ignoring the sightless eyes that seemed to stare accusingly at her, she peered back up towards the crowded trail. To her surprise, a warrior writhed about on the hard surface, mere feet from her. Gravity's assistance was bringing him inexorably closer, and sunlight glinted on the blade in his hand. Although in terrible pain, he had apparently forgotten his instructions, because it was very obvious what his deadly intentions were.

Lucy moaned with fear, but whereas in the past she would likely have frozen, now her response was tempered by harsh experience. The old hag still gripped a knife, and her young killer meant to have it, even though in truth knife fighting hadn't formed any part of her childhood. Yet even as Lucy prised it from unresisting fingers, she doubtfully wondered where to strike her approaching assailant. And all the while his savage compatriots called out their encouragement, although it was noticeable that none of them attempted to assist him.

Then the youngster's dreadful predicament was settled from above. Again the 'Buffalo Gun' crashed

145

out, and the Comanche's skull shattered into gory fragments. Lucy screamed as brain matter spattered over her face, but that was incidental. What counted was that she was still alive.

'Mighty fine shooting, Woody,' her father warmly proclaimed, before hollering over to his beloved kin. 'Lay flat behind them bodies and stay still. I don't rightly know how this is gonna pan out.' Then he dropped to his knees to present a smaller target to the enraged Indians.

Buffalo Head could feel a towering rage build within him. He no longer possessed an accessible hostage, and yet his people desperately needed to break out on to open ground. Surely the few individuals up there wouldn't attempt to take on his entire tribe. After a withering glance down at the skulking child, he returned his baleful attention to the hated Tonkawa, who had undoubtedly led the white men to Tule Canyon. If ever a man needed killing, it was he!

'Tell your masters, if they turn their guns away we will leave them alone,' he shouted, subtly avoiding any mention of the guide's intended fate.

On hearing the translation, Tucker and Clayton stared intently at each other. 'So what do you reckon?' the former queried.

'You're asking me?' the hunter retorted.

Tucker sighed. 'I know I've been like a bear with a sore ass, but it ain't hardly surprising. And Lucy is down there. We've found her, for Christ sake!'

'Yeah, yeah. I know, I know,' Clayton freely acknowledged. 'An' I'm powerful happy for you. I really am. But I didn't only come out here for that. I've seen what those devils have done along the frontier. Just like Mackenzie said, they need to be stopped, once and for all.'

Tucker blinked rapidly, as though coming out of a dream. He had been so obsessed with rescuing Lucy, it had actually slipped his mind that some of these same Comanches had also slaughtered his wife and son. So if for no other reason, there surely needed to be a reckoning!

Turning back to Choyopan, he rasped, 'Tell him to go to whatever he calls hell!'

The Tonkawa duly translated that, before quickly stepping back into cover. The parley, such as it had been, was irrevocably over.

For long moments, Buffalo Head sat his pony in stony silence. He could sense the eyes of all his people on him. As on so many occasions before, they expected him to produce a solution, and true to form, an idea was taking shape. Just because they didn't have the white bitch in their possession, didn't mean that they couldn't still put her to good use. To continue up the trail would cost the lives of many of his warriors . . . unless the white eyes' attention was diverted.

Rapidly, the war chief explained his plan and assigned six men to dismount and use their ponies as shields. Next he told the rest of them to make ready. On his signal, they would need to charge up that trail, as they had never done before. As he glanced over to where the girl was hiding, his thin lips twisted into a cruel smile. Then he gave the order, and his six warriors opened fire.

As bullets smacked into the ground around her, Lucy screwed her slight frame up into a trembling ball behind the corpse. Then a piece of lead struck the old woman's chest, and the terrified girl felt the impact of it with her own body. That was just too much to take, and so she began to scream her lungs out. What she couldn't possibly realize was that the Comanches weren't actually trying to hit her . . . yet. What they needed to do was draw the fire of her father and his companions.

As the dreadful turn of events unfolded before him, Jared Tucker reacted in the only way that he could. Levering in a fresh cartridge, he opened up with a rapid fire on the warriors tormenting his daughter. The ponies protecting them immediately took hits, but the unfortunate creatures could be easily replaced from the vast herd. In support of his companion, Clayton also began shooting, and it was then that Buffalo Head issued his next command.

The mounted warriors erupted into action, viciously quirting their ponies into a gallop. Unburdened by any emotions other than self-preservation, Choyopan ignored Lucy's plight and instead took aim at the nearest Comanche. As his Springfield crashed out its defiance, the fast approaching warrior fell from his pony, blood spurting from his neck. Yet there was no way that a single breechloader could hold back the whole tribe, even on a narrow incline. Clayton also recognized the danger, and regretfully transferred his support. What they really needed, though, was Tucker's Winchester, but he was solely concerned with relieving his daughter of her distress.

Driven by a mixture of anger and desperation, the Comanches uncharacteristically ignored their losses and pressed on for the summit. Clayton's Sharps blew another warrior clean off his pony, but then the rest were through to open ground, and suddenly everything had changed.

With consummate skill, the Indians fanned out on to the sun-bleached Llano Estacado and swung their mounts around. After having been sorely used by the white men's guns, they fully intended to exact bloody revenge. And if they could take either of the white men alive, then so much the better, because savage torture meted out at leisure was something they excelled at.

'If you don't help out, Lucy won't have a pa left to take her home!' Clayton bellowed.

Startled, Tucker swung about and saw the Comanches spreading out around them. Down on the trail, half of the snipers were bleeding out as a result of his rapid fire, but Lucy was still under threat. His dilemma was agonizing, and it was about to get worse. Howling out their traditional war cries, the warriors swept in from all sides. His head pounded with indecision.

Choyopan knew full well what could be expected from their attackers. 'Don't let them take you alive, white eyes!' So saying, he placed the Springfield's muzzle under his chin and began a mournful death chant. Tucker regarded him with wide-eyed horror. Until that moment, he really hadn't considered that he might actually die. And what would become of Lucy if he did?

The sound of the bugle call blowing 'Charge' seemed to come from nowhere and everywhere, all at once. On such desolate, open terrain it was inconceivable that any body of horsemen could have caught the Comanches unawares, but this was exactly what Captain Beaumont's Company had managed. Totally immersed in their struggle with the three attackers, the Indians had completely missed the cavalry's arrival. And now they would pay dearly for such a lethal mistake.

Energized by the thrilling bugle call, the weary troopers galvanized their horses into action, and at the same time opened fire. Some of the warriors briefly contemplated retreating into the canyon that they had just sacrificed so much to escape from, but then Clayton and Choyopan began firing on them from the rocks. Tucker, his awful predicament abruptly solved, was already on his feet, and racing for the trail down to his suffering daughter.

Lucy, although physically untouched by the Comanche bullets, had been turned into a quivering wreck by the effect of their brutal efforts. Now, coated in blood and flesh particles from the two corpses behind which she was sheltering, she could only keep her eyes tight shut and pray for the disgusting torment to end.

Buffalo Head, about to lead the women and children out of the canyon, heard snippets of the bugle call with a sinking heart. It appeared that his worst fear had come to fruition, and all because they had taken a young white girl as a slave. It was nothing they hadn't done countless times before, but never before had it had such catastrophic results. Angrily facing his people, he commanded them to scatter and move deeper into the canyon. Hopefully, the horse soldiers would content themselves with killing warriors and ponies!

Some sixth sense made the chief turn and glance up the fated trail. The girl's father was pounding down it like a vengeful maniac. The man's Winchester crashed out, and one of the three remaining warriors crumpled forwards with a bullet in his side. The other two had had more than enough. With no ponies left to mount, they ran off down the path towards their dispersing families.

As heavy firing broke out beyond the rim behind him, Woodrow Tucker longed to rush over to his cowering daughter and take her in his arms, but a distinctive headdress abruptly claimed all his attention.

'Buffalo Head!' he hollered. 'Will you face me, or do you hide amongst your women?' He had no idea how much of that would be understood, but the challenge was unmistakeable.

Now in effect a leader without any followers, that

individual snarled out an unintelligible response. Then, quirting his pony's rump, he set off from a standing start at great speed. Keen to keep any further conflict away from Lucy, her father ran down the slope towards his hated foe. As the distance narrowed, he snapped off a shot at the fast approaching animal. The result was predictable. The pony's front legs buckled, and Buffalo Head flew from its back. Yet unlike some other victims of the white man, he hit the hard ground in a controlled roll and ended up on his feet, still on the path. The only casualties of the fall were his head-dress and rifle. Although immensely cruel to his enemies, there was no doubting his courage. Seeing that Tucker was levering up another cartridge, he drew the only weapon left to him, a long-handled hatchet axe, and ran directly at his opponent.

Aiming for his enemy's chest, Tucker squeezed the trigger. The only result was a metallic click, as the weapon dry-fired. Empty!

Now possessing undisputed proof that the spirits were at least momentarily with him, Buffalo Head closed in fast, swinging the axe. His opponent had two choices. Discard the Winchester and go for the side arm, or use the long gun as a club. Then suddenly his options were halved, because the Comanche just kept coming. Gripping his gun by the barrel, Tucker swung it just as Buffalo Head made his move. With a tremendous jarring crash, the two very different weapons collided. The axe head struck the Winchester's stock, and then slid down over the breech towards Tucker's fingers. In danger of losing them, he simply released his hold and stepped back. Abruptly off balance as the gun dropped, Buffalo Head awkwardly lurched forward.

Tucker drew his Colt and thumbed back the hammer. 'This is for Grace Tucker,' he snarled, and squeezed the trigger. The revolver bucked in his hand, but a hunger for vengeance coupled with hasty aim meant that the bullet struck Buffalo Head in the left shoulder. Infused with his own brand of bloodlust, the war chief attempted to ignore the painful wound and hefted his axe for another murderous swing. And yet suddenly he no longer had the necessary agility. Backing off a little more, Tucker cocked and fired again. This time a .45 calibre bullet penetrated the Comanche's chest.

'That one was for Samuel,' the white man rasped.

With blood soaking his breechclout, Buffalo Head groaned and sank to his knees. The axe fell from his weakened grasp.

Remorselessly, the revolver was cocked yet again. 'And this one's for Lucy. For everything that you did to her, and were intending to do.'

With a tremendous effort, the chief raised his head and stared at the gaping muzzle. A mirthless grimace spread across his bronzed features, as he attempted to display contempt for the white man's retribution. Yet no words came. Only a bloody froth that trickled down his chin. Then Tucker fired again, and the show of defiance was irrevocably ended.

'Pa!'

Jared Tucker turned to his right. Further up the

cliff side, his grotesquely spattered daughter had risen up from behind the wreckage of the old hag's body. Up on the rim above her, the firing had died down and mounted troopers were clearly visible.

'It's over, Lucy,' he called. 'They'll never hurt you again.'

Suddenly she was on her feet, arms outstretched, sobbing uncontrollably. Holstering his Colt, he clambered up to her and enfolded her in a great bear hug. The relief as he held her trembling body was like nothing he had ever experienced.

For a long time they stood there, oblivious to anything around them . . . which was not altogether sensible with so many hostiles still in the vicinity. Finally they came up for air, and Tucker stepped back to take a better look at her. She had lost weight. Even under all the ghastly detritus, her features were noticeably gaunt. But that could be fixed, once he got her home . . . wherever that would be now. Then her tear-stained eyes flitted past him and she screamed.

In one fluid motion, he drew and cocked his Colt on the turn. What he saw raised the hairs on the back of his neck. His discarded Winchester was now held by Choyopan, who was vaguely pointing it in their direction. Tucker recalled Clayton's graphic warning, but then abruptly remembered something else. The gun was no longer loaded!

'You figuring on doing something with that firearm, scout?'

The Tonkawa peered directly at him as though just noticing him. 'Feels mighty good to hold.'

Tucker smiled for the first time in a long while. 'Reckon you'll be needing some cartridges for it.'

'It is mine, yes?'

'Yeah, it's yours. Just remember who gave it to you, once you've got it loaded, huh?'

The Indian favoured him with a half smile. 'You look after girl better now, huh?' Then he turned and walked slowly back up the trail clutching his prized possession.

CHAPTER TWELVE

Colonel Ranald Slidell Mackenzie bleakly stared through his office window and out onto the wind-swept parade ground. A rogue nerve worked under his left eye, and he rubbed the stumps of his fingers together irritably. There were times when he wished to be entirely alone in the world, and this was one of them. On the face of it there was no reason for his ill humour. Little that he had done recently could provide cause for criticism by anyone that counted . . . including himself. Far from it, in fact. His recent expedition had been a resounding success, and he was irrefutably the high command's favourite officer on the frontier. And yet, here was a man who would never be at peace with himself. Hardly surprising perhaps, considering how he had suffered over the years. His had once been a carefree, agreeable personality, but those days were long gone.

The sight of the two civilians and a young girl walking slowly towards the headquarters building sud-denly claimed his attention. Recollection came to him. The captive child. Captain Beaumont had informed him that she had been recovered. Mackenzie scrutinized her with professional interest. The visible injuries would no doubt heal, except perhaps the nose, which appeared to be permanently out of line. She clung to her father as though never wanting to let him go, which was a good sign. Clearly the girl hadn't been held long enough to have turned Comanche.

As the civilians got closer, he sighed and moved away from the window. It appeared that they were intending to pay him a visit, and he supposed that he would grant them a few moments. After all, it was thanks to them that Buffalo Head in particular could no longer wreak bloody mayhem on the frontier.

Sure enough, a few moments later there was a thump on his door, and Sergeant Major Spikes appeared. 'Those two civilians and a child would have words with you, sir. If you want me to say. . . .'

'Don't try to second guess me, Spikes!' Mackenzie snapped. 'Send them in.'

Jared Tucker surveyed the colonel's hard, detached features, and briefly wondered whether he was making a mistake. Then he felt the ever-present pressure from Lucy's grip, and suddenly he knew that he was doing the right thing.

'I . . . that is, we, wanted to thank you for sending Captain Beaumont on to Tule Canyon. If he and his men hadn't turned up when he did, we'd have been dead meat for sure.'

For a long moment Mackenzie said nothing. He

just stared at Lucy, oblivious to the awkward silence that had descended on to the room. He wondered if the homesteader fully realized the likely extent to which his daughter had suffered in that Comanche village. Perhaps not. Or maybe he did, but preferred to just wait and see. However it all turned out, at least he had her back. And so, finally, he responded, and for some reason he opened up far more than he had intended.

'I deemed it to be the correct action under the circumstances, and so it turned out. Both you and Mister Clayton have performed a great service for the frontier. And it was only right that this child should be rescued and returned to her family.'

Abruptly recalling that her other relatives had been brutally slaughtered before her eyes, he paused uncomfortably for a moment before going off at a tangent. 'As for me, well, it seems I'm done with Texas for a while. General Sheridan has appointed me commander of Fort Sill and its Indian reservations. So who knows, I might find Quanah Parker to be among my charges. That devil ran rings around the US Army for years, but it appears as though he has finally accepted that his place is on a reservation, guiding his people. And he is half Texan, so he may well make something of it.' With that, he fell awkwardly silent for another long moment before apparently coming to his senses and calling out to the sergeant major: 'Spikes, show these people out. I've much work to do before leaving here.'

*

Back outside, Woodrow Clayton shook his head. 'That's one strange hombre in there. If there was anyone likely to end up putting a bullet in their own head, I reckon it would have to be him.'

Tucker shrugged. 'Maybe so, but he saved all our lives, and for that I'll always be grateful.'

Lucy silently tugged his hand. She hadn't uttered a word since leaving Tule Canyon. How long that would continue was anybody's guess. One thing was for sure. From now on there would be no more solitary rides beyond the settlement line for him. All his attention would be focused on getting her well again, and dealing with any product of her captivity. For he knew that Quanah Parker would be only one of many half-breeds born to captives of the Comanches.

'Let's go home, Lucy,' he tenderly remarked. 'Whether we stay there depends on how you feel, yeah?'

She stared at him with great solemnity before finally nodding. Her lips remained resolutely sealed.

'And what's next for you, Woody?' he asked. 'I owe you a debt I can never repay. You know that, don't you?'

The other man smiled. 'Well, I sure ain't no debt collector. And I kind of figured I'd go back to shooting dumb animals. If nothing else, there's good money in it. But rejoining my outfit up near Adobe Walls will take me past your spread, so I guess you can fatten me up some if you're willing.'

Jared Tucker patted him affectionately on the back. 'It will be my pleasure.'

*

A short while later, three riders headed north out of Fort Concho. It was a remarkable fact that the land they were returning to would likely be safer than at any time in the last two hundred years!